Five of Kathryn Mattingly's
tion for excellence: *Cheating Paradise, Goodbye My Sweet, The Stein Collection, Light of the Moon,* and *Morney.*

From the editor of *Writer's Digest* in reference to award winning short story *Cheating Paradise*: "This year's contest attracted close to 18,000 entries. Kathryn Mattingly's success in the face of such formidable competition speaks highly of her writing talent and should be a source of great pride."

Other reviews for Kathryn's short stories . . .

"Kathryn Mattingly's fiction has always shown great depth of character and emotion, with simple, yet clever plots. Her characters live and breathe in my mind for a long time after reading about them. I hope she keeps writing short stories and novels forever."

—ELIZABETH ENGSTROM, bestselling author of *Baggage Check*

"Kathryn Mattingly's story *Half Moon Cay* is wonderful, and very moving. Her stories make me feel as if I am there. *Skyward*, from the reading at Powell's bookstore, and *Light of the Moon*, from Ghost Writers weekend, are two such stories. Kathryn's writing is very powerful."

—JAMES A. BEACH, Editor-in-Chief of *Dark Discoveries Magazine*

"Kathryn Mattingly weaves sensory magic with her words. Whether writing about vengeful ghosts, forbidden love, or motherly sacrifice, her elegant prose offers seamless transport into the lives and hearts of her characters. Once swept away, you may not want to come back."

—ELDON THOMPSON, author of the fantasy trilogy series *Legend of Asahiel*

"Kathryn Mattingly's *Morney* in the anthology *Ghosts at the Coast* stands out as being superb and highly original. It is a spooky tale about a mysterious gypsy girl in Rome."—JONATHAN REITAN, book review in *Dark Discoveries Magazine*

Fractured Hearts

Kathryn Mattingly

Winter Goose
PUBLISHING
where words take flight
wintergoosepublishing.com

Winter Goose Publishing
2701 Del Paso Road, 130-92
Sacramento, CA 95835

www.wintergoosepublishing.com
Contact Information: info@wintergoosepublishing.com

Fractured Hearts

COPYRIGHT © 2014 by Kathryn Mattingly

First Edition, February 2014

Cover Art by Ladd Woodland

ISBN: 978-1-941058-03-9
Typeset by Odyssey Books

Published in the United States of America

for Dennis
the love of my life

every day in your quiet way, you have loved me completely
but the truth to be sure, is simply that I love you more

table of contents

fractured hearts

our minds need only follow
where our hearts are leading
and hope that when fractured

. . . we can stop the bleeding

the stein collection

Kell is perhaps not what we would define as an entrepreneur so much as an opportunist. Nonetheless she laboriously sweats over finely crafted steins which have much to do with the drinking and dancing establishment she owns and operates. The author would share that there really is a Kell's Restaurant and Pub with live music near the waterfront in Portland, OR. A lot of history surrounds the old brick establishment that sees gray rainy days more than sunny ones and still serves cold beer with tall tales on stormy nights.

Sam stood in the rain listening to live band music and the clinking of glassware from Kell's bar. Through the heavy paned window, she glimpsed elbow-to-elbow people on metal stools at a highly polished counter. Shelves jammed with bottles of liquor in every shape and size hung on the wall behind the bar. It was a cozy picture of a patron-filled pub on a Saturday night.

She peered in the adjacent window and saw the restaurant side of Kell's, with its cloth-covered tables carefully arranged. Dreamy piano music escaped from the walls and lingered in the rain-soaked air with bass guitar sounds from the bar. Diners smiled politely at one another, unlike the crowd on the other side where laughs were hearty and tunes lively.

Between the restaurant and bar side of Kell's stood a door. Sam looked through the window and saw a steep stairway. It appeared ominous in this dismal weather. Why couldn't her fiancé Jake have met here as planned? Sam was doubly annoyed with him as she stood there in the rain, hesitating to go in. Did they really want their wedding reception in an old dance hall with a shaded past? Kell's Bar was, however, enticingly trendy and rich with history. As the story went, Kell did away with a few too many customers before being forced to close in 1953. Sam pictured a huge Irishman intimidating troublesome clients.

Closing her umbrella she unlocked the door with an old key Jake had stuck in an envelope and started up the stairs. Lightning struck and ensuing thunder shook the building as Sam climbed the narrow steps. Storms were not very common in Portland, and this was a particularly rowdy one. It made her edgy, but she had to check out the room, or Jake might think she'd been too afraid. She already heard him laughing at her. Proud of himself for planting a seed of fear with his maudlin tales about the second floor dance hall.

Rain drummed on the roof as she paused to catch her breath on the last step. Straight ahead there was a dimly lit room filled with tables and a bar set against the wall. The wooden floor was worn and dull. A woman was perched on a barstool sipping beer from a heavy stein. She looked lost in thought. Was this room available for employees on their break from the restaurant downstairs?

On a shelf behind the bar was an unusual set of heavy beer steins, similar to the one the woman drank from. There were at least a dozen of them, each different and unique, but blending impressively as a collection. Yellow-shaded lamps gave them an eerie glow.

The room was just the right size for a small reception, and Sam liked the atmosphere despite the storm's surreal affect. The strange woman continued to sip on her beer and gaze into space. Sam gathered her nerve and sat at the bar a few chairs down.

"I'm sorry to disturb you, but Jake didn't tell me there'd be anybody here," Sam admitted.

The woman turned her head and looked clear through Sam, who couldn't help but notice the woman's striking features. She was a voluptuous blonde and wore a black calf-length skirt that hinted of long toned legs. A white silk blouse cut impressively low finished the classic look.

"You're no bother. Want a beer?" she asked, with a slight upward turn of her blood-red lips. The crimson shade complimented her creamy complexion perfectly.

"Sure," Sam answered. She watched the woman gracefully slide behind the bar.

"I'm thinking of renting this room for my wedding reception," Sam offered up, hoping to break the icy air between them. "It's just the right size." Sam glanced around again. "I'm sure it would hold a hundred people. The billiard room over there would be great for setting up food."

The strange but striking woman plucked one of the shimmery steins off the shelf. She filled it with frothy beer from a tap that flowed generously as she pushed the white pearl handle firmly. Her blonde hair fell to her shoulders, turning under at the ends in a classy sort of way. She set the beer in front of Sam, and their eyes locked in a mutual stare. This time the woman didn't look past Sam, but focused on her through long sweeping lashes. Her eyes were a soft shade of blue and hinted of sad tales. Looking into them was like trying to find something in a fog. The woman didn't have a young face, but it was far from old. It was seemingly ageless.

"What a beautiful stein," Sam commented, feeling very brunette and with no special attributes to distinguish her wholesome good looks.

The woman smiled. "It's from my private collection. You like them?"

"Yes, very much. My name is Samantha Roberts, by the way."

The woman hesitated and then shook her hand. "I'm Kelly Malone, better known as Kell. This whole place used to be mine. The bar, the restaurant, and this here dance hall." Kell slid back onto her stool. She pointed to the far corner of the bar. "That's where the band set up. Best fiddlers you ever heard. They'd start slow and easy about nine p.m. and by eleven there'd be a dancing frenzy going on."

Sam wondered how she could be the original Kell. It would certainly take a crafty woman to make belligerent drunks disappear forever. "When did this quit being a dance hall?" Sam inquired.

"Long time ago." Kell sighed gloomily.

"When did you decide to rent it out for wedding receptions?" Sam further inquired, but Kell didn't hear the question.

"Businessmen used to flock here when they were in town," she commented. "We had a reputation all over Portland."

"I know Kell's bar is sure popular with the college crowd nowadays," Sam mentioned.

Kell didn't acknowledge Sam's comment. "Most of the men who came here only had a few beers. They'd dance for a little while and then return to their motel rooms or homes if they lived nearby," she said as if in a trance.

"Was there a live band every night?" Sam asked, deciding to go along with Kell's nostalgic mood.

"Wednesday through Sunday. We closed Mondays and Tuesdays." Kell grinned wickedly. "I paid half a dozen girls every night to dance with the men. That was my secret, feisty girls that kicked up their heels. It brought men in like bees to honey."

"Really? Girls danced here?" Sam liked the romantic idea of that.

"You bet. Of course, sometimes the men drank too much and tried to woo my little dancers out the door and to their rooms."

Sam took a long swig of her beer. "What if the girl wanted to go with him?"

"Not an option." Kell slammed down her stein. "I paid them to dance. Not to find a boyfriend or make a little extra money on the side."

"I see." Sam raised an eyebrow as that sunk in. She watched Kell refill their steins from the pearl handled tap, confused about who this Kell really was, and when this dance hall last operated.

"Sometimes," Kell said while staring Sam right in the eye from across the counter, "I had to take matters into my own hands. Not often mind you, but sometimes." Her dreamy blue eyes drifted out the window where the wind howled, slamming rain into the glass. Old beams creaked above their heads. A shiver ran down Sam's back. It was creepy to be here alone with Kell, who was scarier than the storm.

"How did you do that, exactly? I mean, take matters into your own hands?"

Kell ran slender fingers up and down the beer stein as if caressing it. "I invited them to my apartment." She nodded her head toward the back of the dance hall. "Down the back stairs, beside the furnace. The caretaker used to live there. You know, the guy who shoveled the coal and stoked the furnace." Her eyes glowed, as if on fire with past memories.

Sam looked at her curiously. "You'd invite rowdy drunks to your apartment?"

"Oh, I would calm them down first." Kell tossed her blonde hair. "I'd give them a drink on the house. And it always had a sedative in it." She grinned like a Cheshire cat.

Sam tried to imagine Kell shoving a drugged beer into a drunk's hand, and luring him to her private quarters before he crashed in the middle of the dancehall.

"You drugged him? And then what?"

"And then I would let him sleep it off on my sofa."

"How clever of you." Sam wondered if she might be that gutsy one day. She realized running a dance hall must have been difficult. Just like everything is when wine and women are involved, or men and beer . . . and dancing. Rowdy knee-stomping, swing around the floor, heated up and liquored down dancing. It must have been a dizzy delight to see on a hot Saturday night.

Kell slid onto her shiny metal stool and ran a blood-red fingernail around the rim of her stein. The nail polish matched her lipstick perfectly.

"This building takes up a whole city block. Did you know that?" Kell tipped her head and a lock of hair fell across one well-formed cheekbone.

"It's an old brick monstrosity, for sure," Sam agreed.

"I remember when they kept that coal-eating furnace behind my kitchen revved up so hot I'd cook dinner in just my panties and a bra." Kell laughed, and her trance-like state evaporated. Color ran through her cheeks as she continued. "I like a good hot fire though, don't get me wrong. Pottery is my hobby. Nothing like a good hot fire for that."

Sam was amazed. "You make pottery?"

"Sure do," Kell admitted.

Taking a long sip of her icy beer Sam examined the stein it was served in. There was a solid gold edge around the rim, and when she held it up to the light little metal flecks sparkled and winked at her. "Did you make this ceramic stein?" Sam asked, knowing it was an incredible thought.

"I surely did." There was pride in her eyes. Waving an arm across the neat row of elaborately designed ceramic ware, she indicated the stein collection was created by her own hands.

Sam was amazed to learn Kell had a passion for ceramics. Her long slender fingers and bright red nails didn't indicate abuse. It boggled her mind as she observed the steins. Each one shimmered and caught the light, as if little shooting stars were melded into the glaze. "What makes the shiny metal specks?" she asked curiously.

"I melted down old jewelry to get that effect. I once had a steady source of it."

The stein Sam drank from was the only one with a gold rim. "This edge must have taken a lot of melted jewelry," Sam commented.

"A pocket watch." Kell laughed. "Keep it . . . the stein. It's yours. Consider it a little souvenir from our chance meeting on this godforsaken night."

Kell drank the last of her beer just as lightning struck outside the window. Thunder rambled right through Sam's chest as the yellow-shaded lamps went out. The dancehall became dark. Only a steady downpour on the roof could be heard.

"Kell? Are you there?" The hair on the back of Sam's neck stood on end as she stumbled off the barstool, the stein held tightly against her chest, as if to protect her from the pitch black. She made her way slowly to the front stairs.

"Kell? I'm leaving now!" She shouted above the rain blowing sideways into the window, as if it were a hungry wolf trying to enter and devour her. "It was nice meeting you! Thanks for this beautiful stein!" There was no response. Somehow Sam knew there wouldn't be.

Shaking from a damp chill in the air, or maybe from fear, Sam stumbled clumsily down the stairs and looked out the door. Water was backed up from the storm drains, and rushed along the street gutters.

But the gods had quieted. All she heard was live music and cheery voices coming from next door.

Wandering into Kell's bar Sam felt dazed but delighted by the candles lit everywhere and the friendly laughter. They too were without electricity. Drinks were on the house. The storm seemed to have bonded customers.

"Do you always bring your own beer stein?" The bartender asked, grinning.

Sam looked down at the stout mug held tightly to her chest. "No. This was a gift." She looked right into the bartenders green eyes. "From the blonde woman upstairs. Do you know who she is?"

"I have no idea who's up there. What can I get you to drink?"

Sam set her stein down on the bar. "Nothing, thanks. What do you know about the original Kell? Was he a big Irishman?" She longed for the answer to be yes, a huge Irishman with curly red hair and his mama's gift for song.

"Irishman? Nah, Kell was a beautiful blonde woman. History has it she was ferocious about watching out for her dance hall girls." He shrugged while mixing drinks and added, "Supposedly, she had a way of getting rid of troublesome drunks permanent-like."

"So I've heard." Sam began chewing on a fingernail, thinking of Kell. Hers had been painted red, long and pointy, like little weapons.

"Well, I don't know how true the tale is, but they say she drugged unruly clients and escorted them out the door—never to be seen or heard from again. Finally one too many drunks disappeared and the cops closed it for good." The bartender glanced her way and winked. Was he making it all up? Or did the idea of a beautiful blonde serial killer amuse him?

The lights went back on and everyone cheered. The bartender continued his story. "When they cleaned out that big ole coal furnace to put in gas, a few suspicious-looking bone fragments were mixed in the ashes. Sure enough, they were human."

"Really?" Sam stared at her stein.

"Really. Now some say Kell was too delicate to heave a big man into the furnace, but others thought perhaps Lewis helped in exchange for some free bar food." He leaned on the counter, close to Sam. "Lewis was a large black man who shoveled coal in exchange for a cot to sleep on."

The bartender began mixing drinks again, his story flowing like Irish whiskey. "Of course, some thought Lewis was the culprit cooking the bodies after he found them sleeping in the alley and robbed them blind. Burning up the evidence, you might say. And there was a pawn shop around the corner where some thought he exchanged wedding rings and watches and such, for cold hard cash."

"So no one ever found anything to convict Lewis or Kell with?" Sam asked.

"Nope. And one day she got her own just desserts. She disappeared herself. Some think Lewis did her in because the beautiful Kell was love struck by a gent one night and tried to break her own rules. She waltzed right out the door with a patron."

Others at the bar were listening in by now, fascinated with the story. Some smiled knowingly, as if they'd heard the preposterous tale before. The bartender was in his element. Spinning yarn with gusto while serving drinks cold and fast.

"Lewis was said to be furious, 'cause he was smitten with Kell himself. So out of jealousy he did her in on a stormy night like no other. Except maybe for this one."

Everybody at the bar stared into their beer. One little old man drummed his fingers on the counter. Nobody spoke, but several patrons nodded as if they'd been present when it all happened—if it happened.

Or was it Irish folklore, Portland style?

Sam caressed the gold-edged stein. She thought about how Kell mentioned a steady source of jewelry. Was it from the pawn shop nearby? Or from robbing drugged men before she and Lewis tossed them into the fire? The furnace room was right there on the other side of her kitchen, after all. Sam could see Kell pushing with all her might to shove the limp body into the stove, wearing only her bra and panties, while Lewis helped steady and lift the dead weight. Did they sit around her cozy kitchen afterwards, gobbling down leftovers from the bar?

"They say she haunts the place on stormy nights. Hovering and fretting over those steins like she did her dancehall girls." The bartender laughed.

He'd obviously never run into Kell, or maybe she was just a setup, and he was in on it. If it was a joke, it was a damn good one. Kell was spookier than hell. Sam grinned back, said thanks for the folklore, grabbed her stein and slid out the door onto the street. The rain had stopped and the air had a fresh scent. She glanced up at the dance hall windows. It was dark on the second story.

Sam took the metal key from her pocket. Maybe the lights would turn on if she flipped the switch inside the door. She had to see that stein collection one more time. Now that the storm had cleared, she felt braver. Sam had to know if she'd been duped by Jake and whoever else was in on the fun. But the key wouldn't open the door. That was odd. It opened easily the first time. Sam toyed with the lid on her stein. This one got away. In fact, unlike her dancehall girls, Kell had given it away. Glancing up at the second story window one last time, she thought she saw the blinds shift.

Sam stuck the stein protectively in her coat and headed for the car, thinking it might be fun to have her wedding reception in a haunted dancehall, giving her the last laugh. Unless of course, Jake had nothing to do with her unbelievable evening, in which case, unlike most brides, she would pray for rain. Maybe she'd see Kell again, and thank her for the priceless wedding gift.

by the light of the moon

the lives of cats

I remember lookin' at Tom sittin' there lickin' his paws contentedly and thinkin' about when the monstrous black cat first graced me with his presence. He wasn't really my pet. Tom wasn't anybody's pet. He simply became a fixture in the corners of your life as it suited him, before moving on. I knew this about Tom because one day he just showed up. I opened the squeaky screen door on a muggy July morning to retrieve a fat Sunday paper with the colored comics stickin' out in a tempting anticipatory manner, and there he was, sprawled across my porch swing meowing crankily.

I asked him who he thought he was, lyin' there on my porch swing like that, but he only pushed his nose up into the thickly humid Illinois air and squinted his slanty eyes at me. Tom was purring in a most flirtatious manner and was quite receptive to my sensual stroking of his sleek black fur. As if knowing I was a young widow without a soul to care for, he took full advantage of my pampering services.

I didn't have to say *here kitty* twice when laying a dish of cream at his feet. After he'd licked the blue china bowl clean, he claimed the porch as his own for the morning. I felt obliged to give him leftover catfish from Friday night dinner at noontime, with some more of the cream. That was the last of it and there was none for my evening coffee, so I moseyed on over to the market later that afternoon where I picked up a few cans of cat food too, just in case Mr. Tom was still around when I returned.

He was. I all but charged him rent on the front porch after that. My flowery pillows on the white painted slats of the porch swing became covered in short black fur. Tom hollowed out a nest in the foliage by the railing, where sometimes he curled up in a ball and hid from the bothersome busyness of the day. Only in the dead of winter did he come inside to claim my rag rug in front of the toasty fire for long cozy naps. Weather permitting, when shadows of night fell to the ground like heavy dew, Tom was gone. Not to be seen again until well past dawn. As long as crickets were chirping in the thick grass out back, or a frog was heard ribbitting down by the river over yonder toward Lilac Lane, he was nowhere near.

One day a woman from Scarlet Drive came by selling raffle tickets door-to-door for her church. "Where'd you get that cat?" she asked.

"I didn't get him. He got me. Just showed up one day and decided to stay for a while," I replied.

"I had me a Tom like that one." She nodded toward the swing where Tom was perched like a king on the flowered pillows watching her. He did have a knowing look in his sleepy eyes, and was switching and twitching his tail, which was not at all his usual bored demeanor for my guests.

"He went and run off on me one night after a full blown harvest moon so big and yellow you could sort your socks by it. Truth be known he ran off on me every night, but this time he didn't come back," she added, staring at him all the while.

"Tom's been here going on a year now. When'd you lose your cat?" I asked, hoping the time didn't match at all.

"Oh, it's been about that long. How'd you know his name was Tom?"

"Well, I didn't. But he looks like any typical ol' tomcat to me, so it fit."

"Ain't nothin' typical about that cat," she scolded. "Look at him, lying there like he owns the place. That's one pristine pampered animal for an alley runner. Don't look like he's ever met his match in a feline scrape."

"Yep, he's a big healthy one for sure," I agreed. "Did you get your Tom as a kitten?" I asked, wondering if my Tommy had ever been a kitten, he seemed so ageless.

"Nope. My Tom showed up looking for a free meal all growed and sassy, and took over my tiny fenced yard as if he ruled it, sleeping in the petunia beds whenever he wished."

I sighed with relief when she left, and hadn't bought a raffle ticket, hoping she wouldn't come back. I'd grown rather fond of Tom and didn't want to lose him to Scarlet Drive, whether he'd wandered over here from there or not. I decided that my Tommy most likely had a whole slew of homes he'd borrowed until boredom or more pressing feline matters summoned him.

I realized one day he would no longer grace my porch either, lickin' cream off his chin with a long scratchy pink tongue, or batting flies after a good day's napping—just prior to his running off to romp down by the river, slinking between thick reeds along the bank, catchin' any number of interestin' critters for amusement.

I heard once about cats dancin' by the light of the moon. My Auntie Jane told me the story when I was just a child. She said as a little girl she followed her calico kitty one day down to the river. The harvest moon was full and bright, and she knew those riverbanks like the back of her hand, so she wasn't scared at all. When she got to the clearing around the furthest bend it nearly took her breath away, all the cats there meowing long and low to the moon, rolling around in the grass like they was playin'.

And then my Auntie Jane says she must have fallen asleep, 'cause she remembers hearing fiddle music all of a sudden. Coming from nowhere really, but so loud and sweet it made your soul ache. And before she knew it those silly cats were twisting and turning into lords and ladies, looking so fine in their silky gowns and satiny tuxes, tall and slender, every one of them pretty as a picture. They were elegant and all in tune, partnered up and swirling about.

Auntie Jane says she must have been dreamin' there in the dewy grass, exhausted from chasing down her calico pet, 'cause several of those handsome people were young adults she knew to be deader than doornails. One was Carly Canton, who had drowned that summer at sweet sixteen. Carly'd been a bit of a wild one, with long freckled legs and wavy red hair. As red as Calico's brightest patches of fur, Auntie Jane had observed, which might have contributed to the dreamin' and all, she admitted.

Poor Carly was caught by an undertow and everyone believed it was shameful what with her having been drinkin' that cold frothy beer at her tender age. No excuse just 'cause it was hotter than blazes, all the adults had said. *Never, never drink and swim!*

Auntie Jane especially remembered that summer when Carly died, 'cause the calico cat appeared not two days later. She'd cheered everyone up a little, playing with the dozens and dozens of butterflies flitting about in the fields. Auntie Jane had begged *please mama let me keep her* until finally her mama had said *all right then Jane, just quit a pesterin' me!*

"Billy Mosier was one of them lads in the stylish black tuxes, out there dancin' like a jitterbug on a tree stump," Auntie Jane had said. "He'd wrecked his suped-up sports car at not quite nineteen that very same summer. Wrapped it clear around a big oak tree just outside of town. Billy was a looker, and all the girls mourned his death for quite awhile. He had a way about him, what with that dark silky hair fallin' over his eyes." Auntie Jane sighed. "He always dressed in black, from his wrangler jeans to his shiny leather jackets and polished boots. 'Cept in summer. Then he drove the girls wild with his sleeveless tees, showing all them muscles on his big strong arms." Auntie Jane laughed when she told me that.

Can you imagine such a dream where all the young people, whose lives were cut short by an untimely death, turn into finicky felines and frolic about under the harvest moon? To think they became human again for one night of romping good fun down by the river! My Auntie Jane was a wonder with her tales of such silliness. She never lacked for imagination, and yet I believed she had her wits about her more so than those that would say otherwise.

Tom came crawlin' back after the last harvest moon plum tuckered out enough to have been dancin' all night for sure. Lookin' like something the cat dragged in, I told him, but he only closed them slanty eyes to my smart-alecky tone. If I didn't know any better, I'd believe the entire tale Auntie Jane told me, 'cause that tomcat barely woke up long enough to eat for nearly a week. No more roamin' the hot Indian summer nights after that either, just rolling on his back in the dewy grass out front, and batting an occasional firefly.

This particular summer my niece Lillian Landis graced Tom and me with her presence. Her mama done had it with Lillian, and I thought a cooling off period might not be such a bad thing. I offered to take the rebellious teen into my home for a spell. My sister, Rosie, was grateful to send her to me so she could make it through a day without tears and trauma. Sis knew I couldn't keep that child from her evening escapades with all the other teens in town, but I did promise to make the lovely Lillian compromise between cautious conduct and careless carousing.

She *was* a gorgeous sight, that girl. Missy Lil had attributes to match her name, being a delicate child with smooth lily-white skin, glittery green eyes, and a fragile sweetness about her despite the rebelliousness of late. One night I prepared to follow Lil out the door and down to the river, where I'd heard them naughty young folk were skinny-dipping and laughin' up a storm on these hot muggy nights we'd had of late. The river backed up into one big pond by the cliffs and it was there I could see them all clearly in the light of the near-full moon. They were lyin' about real snuggly like and kissin' between drinkin' and smokin' and jumpin' into the water to cool off their sweaty skin. Probably more overheated from all that kissin' than the suffocatin' weather.

I decided right then and there that my niece would not be returning to the banks of the river where sin was runnin' near amuck amongst our wild and willful youth. The only thing keeping me from draggin' her sorry self home right then was the mere fact of rapid waters between us flowin' steady and strong along the banks of my field and the cliffs of her rompin' grounds. By the time I would forge my way to the other side, she would surely already be headin' home.

Oh how I longed to see her lily-white face by midnight, which was our agreed upon curfew, but she didn't appear at that hour, or the next. Finally I called Rosie and the police. They showed up at dawn with Tom, who was dismayed to come home from his prowling about only to find a parcel of strangers on his coveted porch. At noon Rosie and I sat on the swing exhausted from worry. Tom was curled up tight nestled in the foliage beside the porch rail. Nothing was stirring but the bees on the honeysuckle.

A squad car pulled up and my heart near leapt into my throat as the officer approached us. Sure enough our Lillian had been found, her sweet little body all mangled like a crushed flower, fallen over the cliffs by the river. Lots of alcohol was found in her blood after tests determined she had stumbled to her death. Rosie was overtaken with grief and there was nothing I could do to help. My own sadness made me restless as a cat, pouncing on anyone who dared knock at my door for weeks after the funeral.

I had almost forgotten it was time for that bright harvest moon again, until it slowly began to rise one night, the sky all aglow from its shimmerin' haze. Tom slinked off with a decidedly perky prance that evening, his sleek black fur nearly standing on end. *For what*, I wondered? I thought about my Auntie Jane and her crazy story of the dancing cats turning into lords and ladies, takin' on familiar faces of the young and foolish, whirling about in the light of that big yellow sphere, defying their tragic deaths. What nonsense it was, but still, it soothed my aching heart to think that just maybe my Miss Lil could be all footloose and fancy free like that for a full harvest moon, despite the fall that brought her future to a sudden halt.

I snuck down to the river that night, and was able to see every plump ripe blackberry on the bushes along the bank, that moon was so bright. It did take awhile to reach the shore, as I'd near forgotten what a hefty hike it was. Pantin' up a storm I peeked through the reeds and wondered what them teens from town were doing on the other shore, by the pooled up water near the cliffs. I soon forgot about them entirely, as my eyes beheld a feline fantasy. Every cat imaginable was lying about, swishin' their tails and lickin' their paws, as I lay in the cool grass and watched through my bed of reeds. Next I cannot be sure what happened. I suspect I fell asleep from weariness and dreamed the dreams of Auntie Jane long ago. For soon every cat began twisting and twitching about until their bodies slithered into fancy gowned gals and gussied up suitors.

I watched them dance elegantly and became mesmerized by soft melodies on a faraway fiddle. Shadows moved across a voluptuous harvest moon, and kept in motion with the haunting tunes. I dared to believe I saw our Miss Lillian, all titillating in peach taffeta, her emerald eyes set off by the stunning gown. She danced with an alluring young stranger who could have been Billie Mosier, what with his dark tousled hair tumbling over slanty eyes.

I awoke, at just past dawn, with the field before the flowing river clear and void of all movement, cat or ghost either one. Dazed, I stumbled home and slept till well past noon. When I slid open the squeaky screen door to glance about for Mr. Tom, he was nowhere to be seen, but I had to look twice upon the gently rocking swing, for its yellow flowered pillows held another feline now. A dainty white cat lay there all prettily perched upon her back haunches, whining a high-pitched meow at me. I near stared right through her bright green eyes and then quickly went to fetch some cream.

A few weeks later Rosie came by, her first time out since dear Lillian's death. She asked me who was playin' queen, lookin' all pampered on the porch swing. I told my sister I had no idea where that Tom had run off to, or why the fluffy feline now fancied this her home. Rosie asked what was I gonna call the cat, for Tom would never do.

I came and stood beside my sis there at the door and gazed upon the sublime creature that had left her queenly swing every evening to carouse along the river. I shrugged an indication of not having bothered with a name, and Rosie took it upon herself to call the fluffy feline Snowball. 'Twasn't a chance in hell the rebellious bundle of fur would allow for such a silly name. My choice was more fitting, although I was quite careful not to mention it around my dear sister, who packed up and moved to Florida in order to forget her pain.

My new feline friend and I have snuggled up every morning since then on the white slat swing, where I read the daily paper and my delicate Miss Lily drinks her cream. I've seen Tom on several occasions, hangin' about when the shadows fall sideways and evening dew begins to gather. He sits off aways in the distance beyond the picket gate and waits for Lily to finish grooming her dainty little face with her sticky pink tongue. When finished, she bolts from the chair in a most graceful manner and is off with her tomcat, who has come a callin' . . . to roam along the river in search of whatever it is that can only be seen by the light of the moon.

truth

truth is
paradise . . .
when warm
breezy, easy
but seldom
otherwise
it is hard truths
that surprise
make us run
make us hide
make us
cheat paradise

cheating paradise

My view from this room has deeply affected me, like a painting that speaks to the soul through the artist's brush. At first all I saw was the very average and dated décor. When slipping through the sliding door onto the deck, disappointment was further felt at how small the inlet was with its white sandy beach barely bigger than a picture postcard. There were lots of native Hawaiians everywhere at first glance, and although I found them interesting, they were somewhat intimidating. At least, upon my initial arrival to shores more foreign than familiar.

But slowly the view from my deck transformed . . . became interesting, as it gathered personality and depth, just as you did. The cumbersome black lava dock that seemed less than picturesque with its noisy machinery—at second glance—is merely the backdrop for the tiny boat-studded bay. Dock activities upon even closer examination are one intriguing event after another, and never boring to observe from my binoculars.

The sailboats bobbing in the sea beside the broad dock have set my heart to dreaming unencumbered dreams that have no boundaries, no rules to fence me in. There is just ocean blending into sky as my thoughts soar unrestrained.

I have observed the mood shifts of this scene outside my window, created by the different shades of light and array of sounds, just as I know your moods by heart. Each morning a rooster crows in the distance while pigeons coo in nearby palms. The sky glows a soft pink and hills beyond the bay shimmer in a rosy mist. Canoes and kayaks are neatly arranged on the early morning shore, and there is order in the peaceful dawn, where soon there will be chaos.

After the rooster quits crowing and the mist on the hills lifts, people begin to appear on the beach and along the wide dock. Skippers are preparing their boats to set sail, or transport divers and deep-sea fishing tourists to where they can renew their spirits. Each day they embark upon a different adventure, capturing precious moments that will sustain them through stress filled days on the mainland, just as our stolen moments sustain me through harrowing weeks without you.

By midday toddlers run in the shallow waves and lovers lay side by side on towels letting lotion-drenched bodies absorb the mystical powers of a tropical sun. Kneading out knots formed by a career of choice, spouse of choice, lifestyle of choice. Loosening muscles constricted by daily duties that weigh us down and send us looking for where the clock stops. Where time stands still. Where palm trees, sun, surf, and sand merge as one priceless therapy session.

Early evening brings a subtle breeze to lick at hot, oiled skin and clear out semi-conscious thoughts of selling everything you own and leaving everything you are to come here and be someone else, anyone else. The lights begin to glow in the lamps that dot the shore and line the dock of the tiny mystical inlet, or fantastical lazy bay. The harbor changes color like a chameleon, from sea greens and misty blues to shades of melon and peach as a tender sunset caresses the shoreline.

In the middle of the night I lean on the rail and feel as one with this setting, as I now feel as one with you. The sprinkling of lights everywhere give feathery shadows to the palm leaves moving ever so slightly in the balmy, barely distinguishable breeze. Sounds are noticeably nocturnal. Hushed, reverent. Lush greenery rustles—swaying like a whisper, and the tide is but a tiny ripple kissing the sand. Boats in the harbor are moored with creaking ropes that strain against the lapping sea. Silent twinkling stars light hills beyond the bay. Nothing stirs in the predawn but my imaginings.

A morning serenade from the neighboring rooster awakens me. The native birds are quiet, but can be heard in the late afternoon as a frenzied chorus of chirping in the bushes beside the paths traveled endlessly by browned, barefooted beings. I know the routine well—the sights, the sounds, the life outside my railing on this miniature island beachfront postcard, with the long wide dock and glistening sea-blue bay. It is holding me hostage for a fraction of time, an instant. It is a taste of what life can be at its most elusive height of non-reality—just as you are.

I have come to know your sounds—your touch. Memories of you tickle me like a soft tropical breeze. Who you are has melted into who I am, similar to this view, this inlet, this bay of sailboats silhouetting the horizon. You are my paradise. You fill me up with your poetry, like exotic flowers—delicate, fragile, oozing a sweet scent. Luring me in, seducing my senses. Like blossoms on the breeze, salt spray in my hair, your hands on my body. Caressing, arousing—tasting, tantalizing.

Your love is like shimmering colors in the mist, with no hope on the horizon, as we dare to dream beyond where even sailboats boldly roam. I lie near the shoreline where waves rush over me. Foamy, frothy, and glistening as they soak into the sand beside me, as I sink into your strong arms, fall into your mirage of safekeeping from the world. For only an instant—like paradise—fleeting, costly, not obtainable, not really. Not for long. Not forever. Not for everyday tangible touchable reality. Because we have lives to return to, loved ones to protect, lies to tell.

Why do we hide who we really are, what we really are all about? Why do we cling to images and illusions that define us through others, but not through our own eyes? How did fear and deceit come to rule us? What courage it would take to give up the falsehoods we hide behind, to respect others with our honesty. We are cheating those who trust in us to be true, cheating on private beaches with stolen moments.

Cheating paradise.

What could be more foolish than that?

I am sad to leave this room and this view that I have grown so accustomed to. I will mourn the loss of my short stay in paradise. I will never forget the sounds and the moods, the various settings of light and shadow. Like the back of my hand, I know this picture of perfection—these palm trees, lush hills, and sleek sailboats. This harbor will live forever in my mind, only its details fading with time.

But the monstrous dark lava dock will remain crystal clear to me always, because it is part of the real world, the everyday busy working world. It is the link from fantasy to reality, the lifeline that clearly defines the truth of the matter—I cannot return again to your open arms, any more than I can ever forget our time in paradise, our last hurrah, our final kiss, our love that could only leave a wake of destruction in its path.

An illusion of integrity merely makes a mockery of it.

And so the tiny picture postcard of our shared fantasy will sit unassumingly in the journal of my life, and if I could write upon the back and mail it to your door, my sweet, lost, forbidden love, it would simply say that paradise comes with a cost.

And that price is more than I can bear.

dance of the dolphins

a tropical awakening

I couldn't believe how good he looked at five a.m. freshly showered and wearing my favorite shirt. Did he do that on purpose? After dropping our luggage off at the curb, he hugged Paityn and me goodbye and was gone. I stood there with lingering memories of lovemaking the night before, while watching the silver convertible become a blur in the distance

"Let's go, Paityn." We rolled our luggage into the airport and up to the airline gate. Our flight was uneventful except for the anticipation of arrival in paradise. Once there I guided us through the Maui airport on past experience and instinct. After much debate about which car to rent, we headed for Kaanapali in a red convertible.

"You can drive," I told Paityn, when stopping for sunscreen and bottled water.

"What about the 'must be twenty-five years old' car rental rule?" Paityn asked.

"What about it? Our personal insurance will cover us, whether we follow their guidelines or not," I answered, although somewhere deep inside it felt uncomfortable encouraging her to break the rules.

Arriving at the Villas we checked in, upgrading immediately to a nicer room with a full kitchen. In record time we hit the beach, grabbing books and sunblock on our way out the door. As always, the line of vision where glistening blue-green water caresses sun-warmed sand took my breath away. I walked the entire length of beach, leaving my bikini-clad daughter preoccupied with the young hired help in the rental shack, where I hoped she would negotiate a cut rate on renting a cabana.

Breathing in the salty air I marveled at the horizon, dotted with boats of varying sizes. Only one shade of blue distinguished sky from sea. While admiring the sailing vessels my mind wandered to the clean-shaven man that had left us on the curb this morning. He seemed farther away than a six-hour flight. Remembering it was his choice not to come, I quickly dismissed any guilty thoughts. It was time for a Mai Tai.

Paityn was all too happy to tell me she got the cabana free for the rest of the day. A welcoming gift, the cute tanned boy in the rental shop had said. I smiled and nodded as I headed for the bar next to the pool, not far from the rental shack and the beach. Perching on a faded green director's chair at the outside counter, I could see clear through the weathered structure to the sea beyond the sand, and the sailboats on the horizon.

The bartender was as laid back as the Villas. He served my drink with a smile and a happy, "How are your accommodations? You just arrived, right? Because I'm sure I haven't seen you before this Mai Tai. My name is Peter. What's yours?"

I took a closer look at the man with hair bleached nearly white from surf and sun. His eyes were as blue-green as the sea. I wondered what outdoor activity he indulged in to keep his muscles hard and his skin bronzed. He was seasoned just enough to arouse my interest.

"My name is Jordan Weybright, and our accommodations are perfect. Thanks for asking. We just got here a few hours ago. How long have you worked at the Villas?" I inquired, sipping on the Mai Tai as I waited for an answer.

"Ten years. I'm from Portland, Oregon, originally. I booked a flight one day to get away from it all and never made it back to the mainland." Peter quit wiping the counter and gave me his full attention.

"Do you have a family back there in Oregon?" I asked.

"Not really. I'm divorced. Where are *you* from?" he asked, and then added, "Are you here alone?"

His eyes glistened like sun on the playful sea.

"I'm an Oregonian, just like you," I said. "I brought my teenage daughter here for spring break. It's her first year at college and we've really missed each other, so we're spending quality time together. How long have you been divorced?" I knew my questions were prying, but I couldn't help myself.

He smiled and said ten years, knowing I probably guessed that already. Peter took an order and I admired the view of the surf out the far open side of the rustic room. He came back after a few minutes and leaned on the bar, our eyes only inches from each other.

"You ask a lot of personal questions, for a tourist."

"Well, it's just that I'm a legal secretary, used to calling a spade a spade. I spend most of my time on a computer." I smiled my best smile.

"Hmm. Work with attorneys and computers, eh? Well fancy that. I used to be an attorney and I just bought a laptop for Christmas."

"Why? Are you going to practice law over the Internet?"

"I thought I might try my hand at e-mail, for starters. I have a daughter. She's fourteen. Haven't seen her for ten years. Her mother and I didn't part ways in a friendly manner. Kristen sent me her e-mail address in my Christmas card. Said she just got a computer and would love to hear from me."

There was more to Peter than met the eye, I surmised, while pushing windblown hair behind my ear. It was just long enough to catch there and not tumble back into my face. I always wanted to be a tall athletic blonde, but begrudgingly settled for being a petite brunette with highlights. At one hundred and five pounds, tennis was the single sport I excelled at, and that was only because of my two-handed backhand.

"You got her address at Christmas and bought a laptop at the same time, but haven't e-mailed her yet? It's the end of March. What are you waiting for?"

Peter gave me another Mai Tai. "Courage," he laughed. "I don't have the goddamn nerve it takes to do it." He looked directly at me. "How can I be sure she really wants to hear from me? And what in the hell would I say?"

"Well," I sighed, taking a deep breath before continuing, "you could start with, 'Hello, how's school?' I mean, you don't need to delve right into why you abandoned her for most of her young life." It was a harsh response, but I had a feeling Peter needed to hear the truth he'd been denying.

"You're not very delicate with words, are you?"

I laughed. "No . . . sorry. But I'm not always dealing with cold hard facts. Art is my passion of choice . . . transparent silk screens and etchings. Making a living at it one day is my pipedream." I downed my second Mai Tai as if there were fears of my own to stare down. It was time to rejoin Paityn on the beach. Standing to leave I fumbled around for my wallet in the oversized straw bag.

"Hey, Jordan. Is that like the river, Jordan?" Peter's face lit up with a teasing grin.

"Yeah, just like it . . . I guess. Sort of like Peter was an apostle. Not a direct descendant, I'm assuming?" I put my sunglasses on.

"God, no. I may work on the beach but I'm not a fisher of men. Jordan, tomorrow is my first day off in a while. I'll take you and your daughter sailing if you want to come. Maybe you can tell me how to do this e-mail thing. Clue me in on what fourteen-year-olds are into so I don't sound like an idiot. What do you think?"

"Where's your boat?" I handed him a generous tip.

"It's down at the harbor in Ma'alaea. Dock twenty-two. Don't worry. It's seaworthy and I'm a decent sailor. I take advanced divers out early in the morning before I come here. Do you want to meet me at, say, noon?" He looked hopeful, blue-green eyes still shining like spray off the surf.

"Tomorrow's my birthday," I said matter-of-factly.

"Really? It's the first day of spring."

"I know. It comes in like a lion. Suits me. I'm a nocturnal beast, restless and intimidating. Or so I've been told."

"You're a Pisces," Peter said. "Sign of the fish, like the dolphins that come and dance on the first day of spring." He wiped the counter off and began mixing a lava flow for the customer two bar stools down from me. Sweet strawberry syrup oozed over the sides of the tall glass as I pondered what he'd said.

"Dolphins?" I asked, halfway leaning onto the chair I had just vacated.

"Yeah. According to legend they come every year on the first day of spring at one in the morning, and dance at the edge of the surf. They're led by a huge white ghost dolphin. He spits out purple coral as a peace offering to man, sort of a sacrifice. Hoping to live in harmony as one intelligent species with another." Peter was only slightly grinning, a happy carefree I-kid-you-not grin.

"Why purple coral?" I asked, playing along with the fish tale.

"Because it's the most valuable and the hardest to get. It's very deep and far from here. And there's a limited amount of it," he said, tossing his golden hair with a twitch of his head.

"Fascinating." I stood up to go. "If it's okay with Paityn, we'll sail with you. Did you say dock twenty-two, at noon?"

"Yes, great! I'll bring lunch. See you there." Peter began frantically mixing drinks for happy hour customers suddenly arriving in droves.

I found Paityn in the cabana on the beach. She agreed that sailing would be fun. Concentrating with difficulty on my book for the rest of the late afternoon almost kept thoughts of David from entering my mind and tugging on my conscience. David was the blue-eyed blond I left at the airport speeding away in my sports car, while leaving me alone with all the trust it took to make a marriage last as long as ours had. Paityn and I watched the fiery sunset ablaze with oranges, purples, and pinks. Then we lingered until dark, teasing our toes in the lapping surf.

The evening was spent in Lahaina, browsing through my favorite art shops. Eventually we strolled down the strip to Bubba Gump's, devoured a large serving of coconut shrimp, and shared strawberry shortcake oozing in whipped cream. Boats of all sizes dotted the horizon out our window. We marveled at their dark ominous shapes. I thought about the dolphins. What a picture for idle imagining. Beautiful silver mammals limber and agile, perched on the edge of the surf, dancing and shimmering in the light of the full moon. And it would be a full moon. What a shame it wasn't really going to happen. It would be so amazing to witness.

On the way back to the Villas we stopped at The Whaler's Village and admired glistening jewels in exclusive shops. I bought Paityn a virgin lava flow at Lalaini's and downed a couple more Mai Tais. A beautiful brown man with dark curly hair played soft Hawaiian music at the open-air bar. He strummed his guitar and sang songs to break your heart. They were soul searching. Like the gentle surf humming just beyond the sand floor and hedge of flowering bushes.

I tried not to think about sailing in twelve hours with a man I just met and found too attractive for comfort. Instead I looked to the horizon in search of dolphins. I could almost imagine them gliding upright on their strong tails, swaying gently with the surf. A big white translucent dolphin in the lead, every inch of him an omniscient ghost mocking my decisions by his very presence.

We pulled into Ma'alaea harbor, with our convertible top down and our hair sailing behind us. I glanced nervously at the rows of docks, looking for a lean blond man with a seaworthy sailboat. My eyes didn't rest on anything nearing that description as Paityn parked and we began the task of figuring out where dock twenty-two was. As we headed down the second row of boats in slips, we heard a friendly *aloha* and saw Peter waving at us.

"I'm glad you came! Step aboard and make yourselves at home, ladies." Peter's boat was a thirty-five foot sloop. The jib and mainsail were ready to be hoisted as we helped with further preparation, knowing our way around boating like the back of our hands.

"So you're sailors, eh? I would never have guessed!" Peter looked more pleased than surprised.

"Didn't I mention that? There are lots of lakes in Oregon, you know. And the same ocean we share here today. It shouldn't be that much of a shock," I said grinning.

Once at sea, Peter took us to Molokini. The water was so still you could partially see the fish below. Some were boldly striped orange and black, others all vivid purples and pinks. There were schools of sleek silver fish that darted from one direction to another sharply, appearing almost as one large fish with a gentle swaying tail. It was peaceful and protected in the private cove where we'd dropped anchor and lowered the sails to feast on red fin tuna sandwiches, salty Hawaiian chips, and sweet ripe mangos.

After lunch we went snorkeling among the boldly striped and brightly colored fish we'd seen earlier from the deck. The quick darting silver fish slipped between our legs while sea urchins hovered near our toes. Finally we lay on the deck in the sun, exhausted and laughing about our adventure. So absorbed were the three of us in sharing our fish tales, we almost didn't notice a catamaran had eased up beside Peter's boat.

"Aloha! Keegan, how's the fishing?" Peter yelled, as he stood to help a middle aged Hawaiian secure his boat to ours.

"Slow today. The fish are as lazy as the sea. It's been unusually calm waters for March," Keegan answered. "I see you've been snorkeling," he added.

A younger version of Keegan stood with him at the rail. Peter introduced everyone and it was determined that Ty, Keegan's son, was not much older than Paityn. He was taller and leaner than his father, enough so for Paityn to perk up with interest.

"We just saw a group of turtles around the cove here, on the other side. Big ones," Keegan said, as he cupped his hands over his eyes to shade the sun.

"Must be the calm waters today that've brought them close to the surface," Peter commented as he put the dry snorkel gear in a wooden box.

"Wow, turtles?" Paityn's eyes were bright with enthusiasm.

"We could bring your guests aboard and take them around the cove. Lots of snorkel gear on our rig if they want to take another dip," Keegan offered. Ty appeared eager with anticipation, no doubt more for Paityn to come aboard than for viewing turtles.

My daughter looked at me like a begging puppy. "I don't care if Paityn goes, but I'm not up to any more snorkeling," I said cheerfully.

Paityn went with Keegan and Ty, after much reassurance from Peter that his friends were as stellar as my instincts told me. We decided to wait in the cove for them and Peter made Mai Tais to help pass the time. I followed him below where it was cool and a welcome relief from the hot afternoon sun. Peter showed me where I could freshen up. It was a snug room efficiently designed, with a bed built into the wall and covered by a smooth navy blanket. In the opposite corner was a built-in dresser made of matching oak, with three drawers I dared not peek into. Above it hung a mirror. My reflection told me I had been vacationing with abandon.

Scrunching the tousled hair with a tube of gel from my straw bag, and then generously applying moisture-enhancing lotion helped me look less windblown and sun burnt. I finished my attempt at civility with a blush colored lip gloss that tasted like passion fruit, vowing my lips would not be touched, or tasted by passion.

"Great boat, Peter. Do you live on it?" I asked, upon re-appearing at the tiny bar.

"No, I don't live on the boat, but I might as well. You can generally find me here if I'm not at the Villas," he said as he handed me a Mai Tai.

I took a sip of the sweet, strong drink and asked another personal question.

"Do you have a girlfriend?"

"Nope. They seem to come and go with the tide. Do you have a boyfriend?"

"Yes. He also happens to be my husband," I admitted, taking a mouthful of Mai Tai to appease my pang of conscience.

"I didn't figure a woman like you would be available." Peter poured more mix into both our glasses and set the pitcher back on the bar.

"What kind of woman is that, exactly?" I inquired, despite being afraid of the answer I might get.

"Mm, how do I put it? Confident, independent, no fake giggling and string bikini. You don't use your femininity for entrapment, even though you easily could."

"Thanks, I think. Do you tell that to all the girls who come on your boat? Or do all the rest of them giggle and wear string bikinis?"

"Basically. I like to keep life simple. Women like you scare the hell out of me." Peter sat on a padded bench beside the bar as I peered out the porthole.

I thought about that for a minute, while rattling the ice in my glass. I finally got up the nerve to ask, "What is it about a woman like me that scares you, Peter? Is it because I'm not afraid to act intelligent and independent? I mean, shouldn't you be more afraid of the giggling women in bikinis trying to entrap you, as you see it, by being what you want, rather than who they are?"

Peter laughed. "Intelligent women who behave as such scare the hell out of every man. You can bet your rum on it." Peter emptied the pitcher of Mai Tais into our glasses, but I had no intention of drinking mine. I decided a change of conversation might be wise.

"What are you going to say to Kristen on e-mail? Have you thought about it?"

"I think about it all the time. I have no idea what to say. I mean, once I get past *hi* and *how's school*."

Peter and I spent the rest of our time exploring the possibilities of e-mail between an estranged father and a fourteen-year-old girl. I assured him every adolescent woman longs for a father who will tell her she's a princess, and love her unconditionally. That reentering her life was less scary than never being a part of it, and that fears and resentments would melt away as they got to know each other again.

When we were finished, the clock was close to return time for Keegan, Ty, and Paityn, and Peter was close to holding all the rum he could without being incapacitated. I patiently tolerated his indulgence in the rum straight from its bottle, as he struggled with the emotional burden of his mismanaged life, and his reality in the form of a fatherless girl that he must now reclaim as the by-product of a failed relationship with an intelligent, independent woman. No amount of rum could make that easy.

Finally Paityn's friendly captors silhouetted the horizon, and I encouraged my rum laden escort to come up into the sun for fresh air to clear his head. We said goodbye to Keegan and Ty. Paityn told us about her snorkeling adventure with the turtles while Peter sobered up for the return voyage. Our trip back was exhilarating. Trade winds came out of nowhere and tossed us about on the rising swells. With salt spray drenching our faces, we maneuvered the choppy water fearlessly, laughing hard into the wind for no reason at all.

Once back on the dock we thanked Peter for a perfect day. I leaned over and touched his face, as he stood there to watch us leave. "E-mail Kristen, Peter. Do it as soon as you leave here. Sober and sincere." I looked straight into his eyes, as still and clear as the cove we just came from.

"Maybe I will," he answered a little sadly, and then a sparkle returned to his eyes. "If you want to see the dolphins, I'll be there. On the beach at midnight, just south of the Villas by the park." Peter's whole face glowed in the late afternoon sun.

"You're not kidding, are you?" I asked, skeptically.

"Nope. Come on down and see for yourself."

"Maybe I will," I said over my shoulder as Paityn and I walked down the dock and toward our rental car.

"What's he talking about, Mom? What dolphins?" Paityn eyed me inquisitively.

"Oh, nothing honey. Just some old Hawaiian tale about ghost dolphins dancing by the light of the moon and bringing purple coral as a sacrificial gift," I answered, staring at the sea while Paityn drove parallel to it on the highway. I could almost imagine the graceful gray forms on the edge of the white caps, upright and in step with the ebb and flow of the surf . . . a big white ghost of a dolphin out front, looking right at me.

A tropical breeze from our open window awoke me around midnight. It swept tauntingly past my face, leaving a sweet flowery scent in its wake. I could hear the surf beckoning beyond the sliding screen door, and rose to peer out at the well-lit night. A full moon reflected light off the water below. Was everything extra bright, extra vibrant? Or did it just seem that way because I was only half-awake?

Compelled beyond reason I grabbed my sweater and escaped through the screen door, slipping quietly into the night. Shutting the slider carefully, I glanced at Paityn's peaceful expression in the moon glow, dreaming of turtles and no doubt, Ty. Cautiously I meandered through a garden of flowering bushes and rustling palm trees outside our room. Finally my bare feet touched the beach. A roaring surf and cool spray fully awakened my senses.

Walking on firm compacted sand I dodged playful waves along the shoreline while making my way to the south side of the Villas. Peter was near a cluster of palm trees at the edge of the park. He sat on a log, only a stone's throw from where the sea licked at my legs.

"Aloha!" Peter called to me, waving one arm over his head. Sitting down on the log I felt suddenly foolish. What was I doing at midnight, alone with a man I had just met the day before? Clad only in a short, black silk nightie and a pullover khaki sweater, barefoot and boldly trusting a man who told tall fish tales?

"I'm only here because I couldn't sleep, Peter. I love to walk the beach at night. Especially in a full moon. No way am I a fool for you or your dolphins."

"That's fine. I won't say I-told-you-so and you won't need to apologize." He took a swig of what I guessed was rum, straight out of the sturdy amber bottle. Then he handed it to me.

"Apologize for what? Making a fool out of myself?" I took a long swig of his rum, warm on my throat and burning into my pride. "Did you e-mail Kristen?" I asked, wanting to appear saner than my behavior would indicate.

There was a pause, and then a sigh. "No." Peter took another drink.

"Why not?" I took the bottle from him and pushed away pangs of poor judgment with the bite of liquor.

"It's not simple, Jordan. Not carefree and uncomplicated like my life here. When Loren got pregnant, I ranted and raved and denied it was mine. I wasn't ready for a family and a mortgage. I had just put myself through law school. I had a lot of debts. A lot of dreams. I loved Loren, but I wasn't ready for commitment. Not with her. Strong willed, building her own career, her own dreams."

I suddenly realized Peter had been drinking a fair amount prior to my arrival. "Peter, that has nothing to do with now. Kristin's fourteen. Not in the womb." I kept the bottle, hoping Peter wouldn't reach for another dose of denial.

"I know. Don't get me wrong. I married Loren. I loved her and we were happy. Kristen was perfect and beautiful like her mother, always tugging on my heartstrings, always making me crazy with wanting to do right and be right and make everything perfect for them. I worked day and night to build my practice, pay my debts, make a name for myself. After five years, when Kristen was four, I was exhausted, spent, but deliriously happy because I had paid off the last loan, secured the first prominent client. I couldn't wait to tell Loren, who had been begging me to spend more time with them, to make more room for her and Kristen in my busy, scheduled life.

"I was eager to get home, showing up mid-morning, something I'd never done before. I wanted to tell her we could take some time now, have a vacation in paradise. I thought about playing with Kristen on the beach, her blonde wispy curls blowing in the tropical wind. *Let's go thwimming, Daddy.* I couldn't wait to hear her say it, still struggling with her S's. And then I found them together. Right there in our bed. Middle of the morning. Loren and her lover."

Peter stopped there and threw a rock he'd been clutching way out to sea. We couldn't see it land in the dark, but stared after it anyway for a long, silent moment.

"I booked the flight to paradise, alone," he added. "Been here ever since."

Peter didn't reach for the rum, didn't dare. The truth he'd been chasing away with the fiery liquid had come back with a vengeance. I took another sip myself, looking upwards to the sparkling stars, twinkling down at us, winking, blurry, rocking like the rolling sea. Was it the rum? The full moon? I didn't know, my mind a fuzzy swirling indecisive mix of too many thoughts, wandering in and out with the tide.

"You are like Peter the disciple. Denying your daughter three times. Three times Peter denied Christ," I said.

"What are you talking about?" Peter lay down on the sand in front of me, the stars reflecting in his eyes. His head was at my feet.

"You denied the miracle of her conception, walked away from the innocent child, and now are withholding communication from the young woman eagerly awaiting it. Three times, Peter. You've denied what you cherish most, your own flesh and blood. And it's costing you your only chance at happiness."

"I'm not the only one denying, drinking away my fears. So are you, Jordan Weybright. Jordan so bright, so always right. You're running just as fast. Afraid to find the artist within, afraid to be the real you, afraid it will disappoint your man far away . . . too far away in every way that matters. You're keeping life at arm's length. Everything you want is just out of reach, Jordan. Out of reach unless you stretch to grab it."

He sat up in the sand and put his hand on my leg, running it upwards from my calf to my knee. "Jordan," he said in a whisper, "I think I could find happiness with you. I think I'm falling in love with you, Jordan . . . like the river of hope . . . running through my barren desert life . . . filling me with desire.

"Peter, you're drunk. Drunk and rambling nonsense." I let go of the thick-glassed bottle, realizing it was empty as nothing poured from it, not a drop.

Peter's face was a dark shadow. He had the moon at his back and his hand on my thigh, climbing slowly upwards, sensual strong fingers masterfully caressing, arousing. I reached out for his shoulders, putting one hand on each. "Stop it Peter. I'm not your flavor of the month."

He pulled me down onto his bronzed body, dressed sparsely in thin, faded cutoffs. His hands were on my skin beneath the silk nightie, warm and gentle, teasing, daring, inching closer to erotic places. Before I could protest his lips were sealed to mine, tasting of rum.

I bolted up, sitting astride him. "Peter, this isn't going to happen. I can't . . . won't. Rum or not. I belong to someone else."

Peter stopped. He looked sober, serious. "You're not a fleeting moment, Jordan," he said softly. "You're life-blood for my starving soul. I want to devour you, daily, forever. No more flavors of the month. You need a man who thinks you're perfect, already, just the way I do. *Just the way you are.*"

Slowly I moved my hands over his hard chest and the pulsating flesh of his midsection tempting me . . . until suddenly I tore myself from him, and clumsily stood to view the vast open endless sea.

Was the full moon playing tricks on my eyes?

"Peter!" I yelled, not turning or moving, afraid to look away for fear they would be gone. "The dolphins. They're here. Look!" I ran frantically to the edge of the surf and became dizzy, holding my head as if to prevent my rum-soaked brains from falling out and dancing on the sand.

Like the dolphins in the sea.

Was it real? Peter stood behind me with his hands on my waist. His warmth stimulated and dared my desire as I struggled to believe what my eyes told me. There were at least a dozen dolphins, sinewy silver bodies poised as if possessed by a magical energy. Frolicking, flipping, standing on their tail fins. Agile, easily toying with the surf. Silhouetted by a yellow sphere, dazzling, glowing, reflecting off their slippery forms. Whitecaps glistened and spilled over, just in front of the docile creatures balancing on the edge of the waves.

And then I saw it . . . the ghost dolphin, *or was it the shadow of a massive billowing sail blowing in the breeze?* Its bright, gleaming eyes were on fire, flashing amber, *surely not boat lights to warn of their approach?* His body shimmered with specks of moonbeams and shooting stars. Behind the massive ghost the other dolphins wiggled and danced. All together they touched my soul and seared my heart with painful longing. Longing to be free like the merry mammals before me. Free to fail, free to create, transform, become. I felt myself moving, swaying as gently as palm leaves in an ocean breeze. Mesmerized and seduced by the glorious sight. I wanted to join them in the sea foam beside their slick, silky bodies. I could almost hear them calling to me, calling out for me . . .

"Mom. Mom! Wake-up! What are you doing here? I figured you got up early and went for a walk on the beach, but when I didn't see you right away I got worried. Then I saw you here, by this log. What happened? Are you okay?"

I opened my eyes and the dolphins were gone. No full erotic moon silhouetting anything. No sparkling brilliant stars. No huge shimmering shadow of a ghost. No Peter, warm and arousing. Just Paityn, her innocent face tanned and perplexed, staring, questioning. Blue sky. Morning sun. Tops of palm trees hanging far above me. I stood and smoothed my tousled clothes, ran my fingers through my hair. I wondered if Paityn could smell Peter's cologne on me, the familiar scent faintly bringing my conscience into focus, if not my memory.

I did remember rum, strong and bitter, and glanced over at the empty bottle by the side of the log, speckled with shifting, blowing sand. I recalled being entangled with Peter's bronzed, receptive body. His taste. His touch. Just then a wave caught my ankles with soothing, swirling water. I looked down and saw coral. A handful of interesting odd shapes, delicate, intricate. Purple.

I picked them up and let their wetness shine in the morning sun. Then I clutched them to my heart and stared into the surf, where the whitecaps were tumbling, rushing, roaring gently. Dolphins. Were there dolphins? Dancing, gliding, sleek and silver? With a big white puffy monstrous ghost in front of the gentle, frolicking mammals? I envisioned the full moon, the stars lighting up the heavens with a vengeance, a passion. Was it my passion? Was it real? Perhaps I would never know. Perhaps in my heart, I already knew.

Paityn and I had a wonderful week, reading lazily in our cabana, browsing art shops, being moved by island music. Peter was not in the bar again during our stay. He had every twelfth week off, they said, and we'd come in on the last day before his break.

After returning home I spent all my free time in the makeshift art studio behind our house. Afraid to face David, afraid not to face the images within me, begging to spill out onto the silk screens and sheets of metal. Occasionally I glanced over at the purple coral in a jar by the windowsill, and almost saw moon rays dancing on sea foam as sun glistened through the glass.

In June I got two e-mails. Both strange addresses. One was from Peter. He wanted to thank me for giving him the courage to e-mail Kristen. They had since talked on the phone and he was returning to Portland. Permanently. To rebuild his law practice and spend time with his daughter.

The other was from my favorite art shop in Kaanapali, where I had sent my silk screens and etchings to sell on commission. They loved them. Had already sold out of both sets of prints within two weeks and needed a re-order. *I don't know what it is* (they wrote) *about these dancing dolphins. Mysterious, inspiring, tantalizing our imaginations with transparent, shimmering, seducing colors. Everyone's in love with them. We suggest you raise your prices, run new limited editions, and let us hang the first two in our new Sea Life Art Museum. We'd be honored if you would give your approval.*

I immediately ran back to the house . . . to the den . . . to David. I hugged the stunned and staring man, barely able to contain all that I wanted to say about the art, and the legend. My joy was not complete without David to share it with. My island experience helped me to discover that.

Peter was indeed a disciple. Not a fisher of men, but a finder of truth. He caught me in his tangled net and gave me something to believe in. Dolphins dancing on the first day of spring. True love . . . miracles . . . myself.

goodbye my sweet

for want of hidden treasures

Gino watched her silver sports car swing into the scenic pullout and come to a stop not far from his beater truck. Long slender legs exited first from the open door, causing his libido to kick into overdrive. With a wicked grin Tessa approached him, and they locked into a kiss that hinted of the passion yet to unfold in nearby bushes.

But not tonight, he had to remind himself, although it was difficult to bypass the pleasures of her body as he caressed her bare midriff, exposed beneath a tiny halter-top. He longed to run a hand up her thigh beneath the flowery, short skirt, but thought better of it. Gino didn't want anything to sway his determination. His plan was set. He need only follow it to the letter and not let his testosterone sabotage it.

"Just one more week, Gino, and we're out of here forever," Tessa whispered.

Gino hugged her close and cupped her tight little bottom. He gruffly whispered back, "Tessa, did you get the bag of old coins from the rock yet?" He kissed the top of her hair and tried not to think about how sweet she smelled.

"No," she sighed, her head buried in his shoulder.

"Why not?" he asked, annoyed.

Tessa pulled back to look at him. "It's not that easy. I forgot how silly we were to hide them on the other side of the rock wall. I mean, we were just kids, and now the thought of climbing over those old wobbly stones seems impossible."

"Tessa, we can't leave the bag of coins. It's worth a small fortune." Gino tried not to sound overly disappointed that the treasure wasn't in her possession, sitting in that eighty-thousand-dollar sports car just waiting for him to shove in his backpack.

He thought of the legend suggesting the coins stolen by pirates of long ago brought immortality to whoever possessed them. Just what he needed, more than one lifetime of knowing Tessa didn't love only him. Such reality was too brutal to consider, yet it didn't stop him from wanting to steal back the priceless coins he had given her as a young boy sick with puppy love.

Gino wondered if he should postpone his plan, but decided that wasn't possible. This was their last rendezvous by the overhang. He'd have no other opportunity to do what he felt was justified . . . hell, was necessary. He pulled her to him, kissing those sensual lips long and hard, and thought about when they were just kids. He had fallen so deeply in love with her that it hurt. It still hurt, but not nearly as much as when he first realized what a fool he had been to think he was the only guy in her life. Why hadn't he noticed the lustful eyes of other fieldworkers sooner? Those few big, dark-haired blokes like himself that Tessa always brought water and sandwiches to?

He moved his hands up along the shape of her body, felt her full breasts in the braless halter-top one last time, and finally rested them on her delicate neck. His fingers touched the raven hair caressing her shoulders. He ran them through the silky locks as he recalled how wildly excited he had been that day he found the bag of coins. It was in the overgrown vineyard, where they had sent him to cut firewood. Always working when you're a vineyard peasant, he thought, while the owner's kid swam in their private pool and sipped lemonade. But Gino was never resentful until now. He just liked getting a glimpse of Tessa, dreaming that she'd notice him one day.

And then pulling up an old shriveled vine he found the bag. Filled with treasure, it was. Big round heavy coins from a time and place far removed. Even at twelve he knew that. But only recently had they discovered what the coins were worth, and how the pirates had hidden them in the San Francisco Bay. Rumor had it that someone in the

Sorrentino lineage had been a pirate, and brought part of the treasure to the Napa Valley when starting a vineyard here. Gino didn't care if Tessa came from pirates or not. All he cared about was that she want only him, which she didn't.

He tightened his grip on her lovely neck but she failed to notice. She was busily untying his belt, until finally one velvet hand slipped beneath his bellybutton and headed seductively for those pulsing nether regions. He had to quit stalling. In one mighty thrust he lifted her by the neck and pushed her over the railing, watching her puzzled eyes for an instant as she fell down and down, and then down some more into the deep ravine. The Napa River merely trickled along its way here, groping silently past sheer canyon walls until reaching a spot at which it would widen and deepen. He knew that's where they'd find her body, after they discovered her fancy car up at this pullout and pieced it all together.

"Goodbye, my sweet," he called to her, as she nearly reached the bottom. If he were lucky, they'd believe she jumped. Worst case scenario, someone would recognize his beater truck. Then he'd have to lie. *I broke up with her and we parted ways. She must've been more upset than I realized to jump like that. I should've never left her there all alone . . .*

He hoped he could make himself seem choked up if it came to that. And he would be of course, because he loved her with all of his heart, which had made the thought of sharing her with other men unbearable. And then there was the fact of how she was using him to get away, to escape her tyrannical father and be free at last to do as she pleased. Gino understood finally how he was merely her ticket out, her transportation to Italy, where he still had family they could stay with. But even there Tessa would find other men to flirt with.

A few weeks later Gino stood perfectly still as the long procession of cars made their way slowly down the private road. They had emerged from the mansion where Tessa was laid out in a closed casket, after her remains had been discovered in the Napa River, where it swells at the end of the steep canyon. He stared at the rows and rows of straight fertile grape vines waving gently in the breeze beyond the cars, and tried to ignore the tears he couldn't seem to stop for his sweet dead Tessa, whom he'd always love.

He wished she'd felt the same, wished she hadn't pushed him to do such a desperate thing, but he'd rather have her dead than share her. Gino glanced at his peers, their sweat soaked bodies erect as the line of vehicles went by. He tried not to notice those few young bucks that Tessa had taken a liking to.

No one asked him about the incident on the scenic pullout where Tessa had fallen to her death. It was assumed that she had jumped. No one knew why, but they suspected her demanding father had laid the law down about her spending time with his laborers, instead of those more appropriate young suitors from neighboring vineyards. Such an argument with her old man, combined with the discovery of her pregnancy still hidden in its first stages, would explain jumping to her death. Gino didn't know for a fact that Tessa had been unfaithful to him, but he hated how she made him suspect it nonetheless.

Much to Gino's relief, after every last grape was picked, the field hands received their annual invitation to the Harvest Celebration on the grounds behind the mansion, despite the close proximity in time to Tessa's death. Tradition had it that when the harvest was in, hired hands could eat, drink, and dance to their hearts content. He would find a way to sneak over to the far side of the grounds where he and Tessa had shimmied up the old stone wall and shoved the bag of coins in a space between two mortared rocks on the other side.

As luck would have it the young homeless girl, taken in by the Sorrentino's shortly after Tessa's death, had taken a shining to him. The child looked to be no more than ten, and stuck to Gino like glue from the moment he arrived, watching furtively as he gulped down his first glass of tart new wine.

"What's your name?" she asked, staring up at him with a shy grin.

"Gino," he smiled back, recalling how this little Jasmine had awakened among the grapevines in the upper field, and then walked along the rows of grapes until someone approached her. She was dazed and dirty, with stringy hair clinging to her tear stained face. She claimed not knowing who she was. One of the field men took her to the big house on the hill. Before anyone knew anything Mrs. Sorrentino had taken her in, and given her a name and bedroom just down the hall from where Tessa had slept. Authorities were looking for leads, but so far there was nothing. And now here she was sticking to Gino like a fly on a horse's back.

"What's your name?" he asked, already knowing but letting on like he didn't.

"Jasmine, at least now it is. I don't know what it was before," she answered, without the least bit of remorse. "Miss Lydia says I'm like a breath of fresh air in the house, that I remind her of the jasmine bushes in her garden." Jasmine's eyes sparkled. "Their tiny pink buds are the first sign she has of spring."

"Is that right?" Gino asked, thinking that Tessa's mom, whom Jasmine referred to as Miss Lydia, must surely be desperate for a reason to live, since her beautiful daughter was dead. He could only hope the money from selling the old coins would help him lick his wounds of lost love for the next fifty years.

Gino recalled the time long ago when he had first decided to give his newly found treasure to Tessa. All he could think about was how pleased she would be, and how he'd finally stand out from the other boys who worked the fields.

As Jasmine rattled on about unimportant things, his mind escaped back to that first kiss. It was on the cheek. Tessa was very pleased indeed with his gift. Her little cherry lips had grinned seductively, despite her only being eleven. Those clear blue eyes had penetrated his own until he had to look away for fear that she would read his thoughts, and know how much he wanted her for his own, even then.

"Wanna go for a walk?" the child asked, bringing Gino back to the present. He thought for a minute, and then responded yes indeed, he did want to go for a walk. Perhaps this little cherub from nowhere would be helpful in retrieving Tessa's bag of coins. He would buy Jasmine's silence by giving her one.

Hand in hand they crossed through flowering bushes and fields of grass, all the while Gino thinking how perfect to have the child as an excuse for his wandering. Soon they reached the stone wall that ran across the property line to the front of the vineyard. He could almost hear his and Tessa's voices of long ago as they hid the leather pouch in a place impossible for anybody to stumble upon.

"Jasmine," he began, "a long time ago, when I was your age, I used to come here with Tessa. Do you know who Tessa was?"

"Of course. That's the lady who drowned in the river before I came." She grinned widely and Gino thought for an instant she resembled the beautiful dead Tessa with her full red lips and raven hair. He felt another twinge of regret for the way things had turned out. It seemed not long ago that he and Tessa herself had stood here and contemplated climbing this wall, with the ravine far below, precariously awaiting a single slip on the other side.

"She was Miss Lydia's little girl," Jasmine added, her grin reduced now to a coy smile, her eyes slightly saddened but still bright and blue. Gino was suddenly struck by the attractiveness and endearing nature of this sweet homeless creature. Perhaps he should have paid more attention to all that she rambled on about earlier. It might have helped him understand her better, for certainly she was no simpleton. His curiosity about Jasmine was growing steadily by the minute.

Gino knelt beside her and spoke softly. "Well, I found some buried treasure one day, right here on this estate. A leather bag filled with old coins. I gave it to Tessa. We climbed this wall and halfway down the other side to shove it into a space between two stones for safekeeping. But now the wall might not hold my weight."

He paused and let this information sink into her pretty head.

"I see. Well, is the treasure still there?" she asked sweetly, while staring at the wall and cupping her eyes from the sun.

"I believe it is, at least, I hope it is," Gino answered. "If you're brave enough to shimmy over this wall for me, I'll give you one of the coins in the bag."

"Really? To keep?"

"Absolutely."

"Cross your heart and hope to die?"

"Cross my heart and hope to die." Gino made the heart crossing gesture with his right hand.

"Okay! Let's do it!" Needing no further encouragement Jasmine began to climb the wall, with Gino right behind her. When they reached the top, both stared silently at the canyon below. A breeze cooled their hot faces. Sounds of rushing water were all they could hear. It drowned out the laughter and music from the party on the other side of the manicured grounds.

"It's scary up here," Jasmine admitted, glancing behind her at Gino.

"There's nothing to be afraid of." He shouted above the wind and rushing water echoing up the canyon. "Let me see if I can reach far enough over," he suggested, moving along beside Jasmine. He straddled the wall, little stones and old mortar falling away as he did so. Carefully Gino lowered his body onto the other side, thinking Tessa had been wrong. It wasn't hard to do at all, no harder than the effort he made to put the pouch between the rocks in the first place.

Jasmine rested her arms on top of the wall and watched him, her blue eyes filled to the brim with admiration for his bravery. Ever so carefully he reached down and groped the stones that surely held the coins wedged between them. Soon he felt the leather pouch! Barely able to grip it, Gino slowly tugged until it came free. He stood back up and showed the bag to his new little friend. Jasmine giggled gleefully and clapped her hands. But then a rock slipped from beneath Gino's feet and he had to hang on for dear life, tossing the bag to Jasmine.

"Hold the treasure tightly," he instructed while concentrating his efforts solely on climbing back over to safety.

"No problem," Jasmine answered. "It is after all, *my* treasure," she added, while pushing him mightily with all her weight. Teetering for an instant on the edge of the wall Gino stared at Jasmine. Something about her was so familiar, as if those clear blue eyes reached all the way to another soul . . . all the way to Tessa. Yes, it was his Tessa that he saw there in those eyes, as he lost his foothold and tumbled to his death.

"Goodbye, my sweet," he heard the child say as he fell down and down, and then down some more to the rushing Napa River below. His final thoughts were not of his undying love for Tessa, but about the legend of immortality for whoever possessed the coins.

It must have been true after all.

fantasy

in my head
i am holding you
in my arms
in my heart
i am aching for you
in my reality
i am living
in my recent past

your thoughts
your smile
your gentle touches
are more real
than anything I know
you are but a dream
a mere fantasy

our time spent
together
haunts me now
and always will
for I have
known your magic
and it has
transformed me

morney

I've come to Italy to nurse my wounds, having lost another child and knowing it will be my last attempt to bear children. My doctor and friend, Grant, tells me that it takes more courage sometimes to give up and accept fate, than to try and change it. He's lent me his late aunt's house here in Rome, near the *Piazza Navonna*, to help heal my frazzled nerves, which have made me painfully thin. Each morning after a sleepless night I carelessly tie my blonde hair in a ponytail, throw on my jeans and a sweater, and sit at this outdoor café in the *Piazza*.

I silently pray the late April sun will warm my numb heart as I sip on a cappuccino and think about the children I will never have. I cry behind my sunglasses and wipe away tears before they can escape down my cheeks. On my third day of this ritual that does not soothe my agony, a young gypsy appears out of nowhere. I think surely she is an angel, with eyes as dark and deep as God's richest earth, and curls the color of mahogany bark. She peers up at me while holding an enormous white cat in her arms.

"Have you some change?" she asks.

Her English is decent and I find myself charmed by her confidence. The round eyes stare at me innocently. A little red tam on her head matches the plaid woolen skirt she wears. I think she looks more like a porcelain doll than a beggar, for her skin is pale and undernourished.

"I do have change," I tell her, "but why don't you sit with me a minute and talk?"

Her dark eyes look puzzled as she nervously pets the cat.

"I'll buy you some milk, if you'll just sit for a while," I plead.

After a glance in each direction she sits down and the cat lets out a mournful meow. It jumps from her arms and crouches under the metal chair. The gypsy child doesn't appear at all concerned that her cat will bolt. And it doesn't. The feline begins to lick its paws contentedly.

"What's your name?" I ask boldly.

"Morney," the gypsy angel says.

"Is that Italian?" I inquire.

"No. My mama is American. Her mama was a Morney, until she married Grandpapa. I think Mama misses them . . . her family in America."

I ache for her soul that is wise beyond its years. "Is that why you speak English?" I ask.

"Yes, Papa does not speak it."

A waiter appears, and I order milk for my little friend. The waiter looks skeptical, with one brow arched. I look him straight in the eye, even though he can't see my eyes behind the dark shades. He nods and leaves quietly.

"Well, it's a beautiful name. Where did you get that big fluffy cat?" I sip the cappuccino, never taking my eyes from her thin, angelic face.

"She *is* fluffy, isn't she?" Morney swells with pride for her enormous feline friend. "I find her one day, making screechy noises. Poor thing . . . so tiny, and starving."

Not unlike this child before me, I think to myself, as she turns her head of tangled curls and points toward the cobbled street behind us.

"There, in the side street. That's where she was. Papa let me keep her." Morney looks at me, her eyes serious. "But now he says she is too big and eats too much and I must take Chintzy to the cat place."

"The cat place?" I ask, amazed.

"Yes . . . in the ruins, where Caesar died. It's not far from here."

"Why do they call it the cat place?"

"Because there are many, many cats. Maybe a hundred." Morney reaches under her seat and pets Chintzy while the waiter places a glass of milk in front of the child and disappears, not a smile or a word crossing his lips. After one gulp, she stares at the saucer beneath my cup. I offer it to her and she pours the milk into it carefully, placing it in front of the beloved pet. Morney is kneeling beside the chair, and I smile at her red knee socks and little loafers. Someone has mindfully kept this enticing lure for pity from becoming too shabby.

Every day she comes, holding her large white cat, all the while stretching her hands out from beneath the feline to receive coins. The rich tourists at the cafés along the Piazza ignore her and I marvel at how they can be so complacent. Who could resist giving change to this brave little struggling spirit, a mere ghost of a child, with dark shimmering eyes and messy curls beneath a red tam?

I find her scrappy courage contagious, and somehow the pain of my loss is less suffocating. After nearly two weeks of this daily ritual with the child and the cat and the milk, the gypsy angel comes on a warm sultry morning without Chintzy.

"Papa took her to the cat place," she moans sadly. "He says she drank the little bit of milk we had for my sister Lydia." The stoic child hardens her eyes rather than cry. "I will visit Chintzy, every day maybe."

"I'm so sorry, Morney," I mutter, thinking how often I have heard these words myself, and not found them helpful.

"I hate begging!" Morney announces. "But if I do not beg . . . then Lydia will have no milk, even though the milk is made bad with the drugs." Her tone is sharp with anger.

"Lydia has drugs in her milk?" I ask, bewildered.

"Yes, it is to make her sleep, so Mama and Papa can beg and she will not cry. I wish . . ." she confides in me, "one day to have many coins, so many, I never will beg again. Then Lydia can have milk that is not drugged, and she can be like other babies, shopping with their mamas."

I nod, unsure of how to respond. "Perhaps one day, Morney, you will grow up and earn money in one of the shops where you see the mothers with their babies."

"Perhaps," she replies, and leaves hurriedly without touching her milk.

One day Morney brings her baby sister in a carriage that is tattered and worn, and asks me to care for her because her mother is too ill to beg and her father has not returned from the bars. Nervously I look about, and see not a soul taking any notice of this battered pram housing a dark-haired darling like her sister. Hesitantly and with many misgivings

I concede and tell Morney I will watch Lydia while sipping my cappuccino. But she must return for her by midmorning. As my little gypsy friend runs off into the cobbled side street of the Piazza, I see a woman looking sickly and frail, well beyond her years, looming in the distance. I wonder if she is Morney and Lydia's mother.

Amidst odd and perplexed looks of pedestrians strolling by and café waiters gawking at my table, I study the little one placed in my care. She never opens her eyes fringed with curled lashes. Lydia's face is round and smooth like Morney's, another cherub with mahogany hair, and I wonder if her eyes are as dark as her sister's. When no one comes for her, I reluctantly stroll the sleeping Lydia across the Piazza and ask about her family in the shops. In one store on the corner of the narrow cobbled street someone knows her parents. The shopkeeper tells me the father and mother have probably run off, because the father is wanted for killing a man in a bar brawl.

"Roberto is a violent one, when he has been drinking." The little man uses heavily accented English. "He and that woman Isabella are like shadows of the night, always working the back streets."

The shopkeeper tells me he hopes they will pay for the crime, having shamelessly overdosed their young daughter, addicted to the drugs almost since birth. I anxiously peer down at Lydia, but she is waking up from her drug-induced sleep. I can't help myself as I reach for her, to cradle the toddler in my arms. She is so light I wonder what there is of her beneath the shabby blanket.

The storekeeper stares painfully at the baby and tells me it will also die from the drugs in the milk, which are too strong. "Roberto and his woman have less sense than most." He shakes his head sadly. "They are so young, and the mother . . . she takes the drugs. But Roberto . . . he is just a thief and a drunk."

"What do you mean," I ask, looking at him puzzled and confused. "Is this not the child you feared was overdosed? See . . . she's fine!"

"No. Not that one, not yet anyway. The other one, with the cat."

"*Morney?*" I whisper, staring helplessly into his bushy-browed eyes.

"Yes . . . that's her name . . . Morney. She is dead a year this . . . this month I think."

"But how can that be?" My mind races backward. I remember the pale woman in the shadows, the blank stares of the waiters and their non-recognition of my little gypsy friend, who has visited me every day for two weeks, begging coins while stealing my heart. I remember Grant telling me I have hallucinations because I am not well . . . the drugs, the tests, the pregnancies, the lost babies, the strain of it all. I must take a long vacation. And now this, discovering Morney has died well before she could have brought me her sister Lydia this morning.

I decide to leave Rome. I will reside in Milan. There is nothing to return to the States for. Unsuccessful pregnancies have taken their toll on my marriage. Before I go, I visit the cat place Morney spoke of. It is indeed a refuge of partially restored ancient ruins, right in the middle of the city—one story beneath ground level. The whole area is overrun with cats of every size and shape. The felines vary widely from fat and sassy to haggard and frail. A big white cat sits like a queen among them and it is Chintzy. I am sure of it. Dusk is settling in and the lights play tricks, but I swear that in the shadows I see Morney, in her red tam and plaid skirt, waving at me. She is kneeling by the huge white cat, stroking its soft arched back with her free hand.

Racing down the cement steps with her sister still in my arms, I shout out . . . *Morney* . . . but only the cats respond, with wild guttural meows. Sitting down on a large stone in the ruins, there among the whining, growling cats, I cry into Lydia's mahogany curls. We sit for hours in the darkness, huddled together for warmth, but Morney never reappears.

At home now in Milan not a day goes by I don't think of the little ghost-child and her huge white feline. But thankfully, the voices and illusions within me have not come again. And I have a daughter who needs me, since her father was imprisoned for life, and her mother is dead of malnutrition . . . or perhaps a drug overdose. No one could be sure. But I am sure of one thing. It was Morney who brought me Lydia, an orphaned gypsy no more, but a child of my own at last.

desperado

a coming of age story

Bella stood among the marigolds and stared at the chestnut stallion. She had done this many times before, but today was different. It was her sixteenth birthday and she had questions that needed answers. Leaving the marigolds and asters where she'd been digging, she leaned against the white board fence.

"What does Desperado mean, Nana?"

Peering up from beneath a floppy hat Nana answered, "It means outlaw, child. Something bold and reckless."

"How did he get a name like that?" Bella kept her gaze on the big horse with three white stockings and a star blaze.

Nana sighed, rose from the flowerbed, and began gathering pots to put away in the shed. "When he was a yearling he would open the meadow gate and lead all the horses into the upper pasture." Nana chuckled as she reached into her apron pocket for a hanky to wipe her sweaty brow. "They'd be along the rim of the canyon in the morning and your father would have to herd them back down. Took three times before he figured out it wasn't a person leaving the gate unlatched."

Nana stared at the horse. "One afternoon he saw the young thoroughbred flip it open with his slender nose and lead the rest out. He came back and said the yearling was a desperado among the herd, and the name stuck."

"How did he end up being my mother's horse?"

"Your father told her she could have whichever yearling she wanted to break, and she picked Desperado. That's right before she died." Nana shook her head. "So sad to lose your mama when only eight years old,"

Nana mumbled, while still gathering pots. She turned toward the shed, carefully maneuvering through the geraniums.

Bella climbed on top of the fence and watched the horse dance around the meadow. Desperado came close enough for her to hear his heavy breathing. She inhaled his earthy scent that hinted of hay stubbles mixed with sweet alfalfa. Across the field an orange sun slid down over the ridge behind him. The stallion pawed the hard ground and looked right at her.

"I want to ride him."

Nana left the pots and walked over to the fence. "No, child. Your father will never allow it. You know that, *Isabella.*" Her tone was scolding.

"Desperado didn't kill my mother. The wolves in Echo Canyon killed her." Bella got an eerie feeling as Desperado held her gaze.

"A rock killed her, honey. She fell from the horse and crushed her skull on a large stone." Nana paused, observing the curiosity between child and horse. "Desperado kept wolves away on that sad, sorry night your mother fell to her death. And probably they are what spooked that horse in the first place. The wolves in Echo Canyon are famous for preying upon every living creature who dares to go there. You already know that. It's why you are forbidden to ride in the canyon."

"How did Desperado keep away wolves?"

Nana looked thoughtful. "Well, to hear your father tell it . . . when he went looking for your mother . . . he found her lying lifeless on the rocky canyon floor, with Desperado at her side." She slowly untied her hat and took it off, the sun nearly set in the pasture behind the tall, lean horse. "He was rearing up at the wolves and prancing around his fallen princess, protecting her from the pack. The wolves scattered when your father shot his rifle into the air."

"I bet Father will let me ride him. I'm sixteen now, Nana. I'm old enough."

"You can ask child, but he won't budge. He's always been a bit suspicious of that horse since he discovered the gate trick. And then after your mother's accident . . . well he obviously respects the animal, but he's never going to let you get on that stallion, Bella. You mark my words."

Nana walked slowly to the house and Bella climbed down from the fence. Desperado pranced around in a circle and stopped just out of reach. Bella wished he were close enough to pet. She wanted to touch his white star, stroke his proud neck. "I'll be back, Desperado," she whispered it into the wind as she ran toward the house.

Nana prepared a festive dinner to celebrate Bella's birthday, complete with a scrumptious chocolate cake and sixteen lit candles. When she brought it into the dining room with a big smile, Bella's father and Nana sang, while Bella made a very special, secret wish. It wasn't about Desperado. Bella wished with all her heart that she could see her mother again. Somehow, while feeling more grownup and independent than ever, she needed and missed her mother even more than usual.

"Do birthday wishes really come true?" she asked, knowing the answer. This was the first time Bella thought such wishes were nonsense, yet it was the one wish she wanted to come true more than anything.

"Of course they do!" Nana proclaimed. "After all, you don't turn sweet sixteen but once. Surely special magic is involved." They all laughed, and then Bella's father presented her with a tiny box. A gold ribbon shimmered on top, and it looked almost too pretty and grownup to open. Inside was a beautiful silver necklace that belonged to her mother. Nana oohed and aahed over the treasured gift, while the teenager put it on and looked in the hall mirror.

It felt a bit odd to wear her mother's jewelry. Bella wondered if her father had given it to her mother for a special occasion, but seeing his pained expression, she dared not ask.

"It looks beautiful on you, *Isabella*," her father said softly.

"Yes, indeed," Nana barely uttered.

Later that evening, after Nana retired to her room for the night, Bella sat in a chair next to her father. A fire blazed at their feet beneath the stone mantel, for evenings were still quite chilly on the ranch in early

June. Her father stared into the crackling flames, and then looked up to observe the necklace proudly worn around her neck. Bella wanted to ask so badly if she looked like her mother. But such questions stuck in her throat.

"Well, Bella, how does it feel to be sixteen?"

Bella thought for a minute. How did it feel to be sixteen? Restless, curious, ready for more than life had been offering. "I want to ride Desperado."

Her father's tall frame tensed in the leather chair. She wondered what he was thinking. She should have brushed her unruly blonde mop into a fresh ponytail and changed out of her cutoff jeans for dinner. She scolded herself for not doing so. That might have made her look older to him now, and she wanted to look as old as she felt . . . she wanted to look mature, responsible . . . ready to ride that stallion.

"Bella, you *have* a horse. Cocoa. Desperado hasn't been ridden for eight years. He was barely broken when your mother . . . well, when your mother rode him last."

"That's why I want to ride him, because the horse was Mother's. And he likes me. I know he does. He comes up to me in the meadow and looks me over." Bella suddenly felt foolish about her inexplicable desire to ride the stallion. "Cocoa is too tame for me," she added defensively. "I've outgrown the mare."

Her father's eyes widened. Was she a disappointment to him? Too much like her mother, or perhaps not enough?

"You can't ride Desperado. Do you hear me, Bella? I simply forbid it!"

"I'm not a little girl anymore, Father. I should be able to ride my mother's horse," she nearly shouted. She wanted to make her father see that she was capable. She wanted him to stop smothering her with overly protective love.

"I realize you're no longer a little girl." His tone was softer, his words measured. "But you're not thinking clearly. That horse, Bella, has grown wild . . . untouched by human hands for too long. What makes you think he would let you ride him?"

Bella didn't answer as she stared into the fire, its flames dancing lower by the minute. A need to be taken seriously was burning hot within her. She forced herself not to leap from the room and fly to the meadow where she believed Desperado would let her ride away into the night with him.

"If you want a more spirited horse, you may have one," her father conceded. "Choose whichever gelding or mare from the barn that you wish. Choose one that is Desperado's offspring. Is that a fair enough compromise?"

Bella turned from the fire and looked into her father's eyes. She saw pleading there. Guilt sprang up into her chest and restricted her breathing. Her father had always been kind and loving. He always made her feel safe. And she knew she had been difficult lately, discontented, prancing and pawing like Desperado.

"Thanks, Father. I'll think about it." Bella rose and hugged him tightly. She wanted to push him away, out of her life, and at the same time hold onto him forever. It was an odd struggle, like so many struggles within her lately.

"Goodnight," she mumbled, and headed upstairs to her room, just as she had every day of her life that she could remember. But tonight would be different. Tonight she would begin to make her own decisions.

At exactly midnight Bella threw on a sweatshirt and jeans, and stole back down the stairs. She slipped through the back door of the screened-in porch, its creaking hinges hidden by the raspy drone of a million crickets. With a light foot she stepped into the garden through the white picket gate, and crossed the beds of napping flowers to the high plank fence on the meadow side.

The night air was fresh and cool. Bella breathed in the pasture scent of dewy grass and wild onions. She admired the full moon. It seemed to be wishing her a happy birthday with its warm glow. Bella pulled a carrot from her pocket, stolen from the kitchen on her way to the porch.

"Desperado," she whispered, "come here boy." Bella whistled, staring across the dark field. There was no sign of the stallion, but she was not discouraged as she walked along the fence to the shed. Bella opened the door and glanced around nervously before entering. Pulling out a flashlight from under her sweatshirt, she moved its beam along the shelves against the wall. There it was, her mother's bridle and saddle. These were what she had ridden Desperado with until that fateful day in Echo Canyon.

She ran her hands over the smooth leather and wondered what it would be like to ride with an English saddle. She could do it. She knew she could. Bella worried about the bridle not having a bit, but only for a second. She hated bits anyway. This would be a great adventure, this rite of passage from childhood.

Bella put the flashlight down and lifted the saddle from where it straddled the shelf. It was surprisingly light. She threw the bridle over her shoulder and exited the small shed, creeping slowly back along the fence to the meadow gate. Bella shivered at the craziness of her plan, at the lust for adventure awakened within her.

Climbing the white board fence, she called to the stallion, "Desperado, come here boy, I have something for you." Low and steady she spoke to the field of tall grass, over the hum of crickets, into the yellow sphere of the full moon. And then she heard him, heard his deep whinny, his measured gait drawing near the fence. She held the carrot at arm's length, her heart beating wildly. Desperado stood just out of reach and sniffed the air. He stomped the ground and tossed his head, sending his reddish mane flying. Bella didn't dare to breathe.

Slowly the thoroughbred nudged his way forward until his nostrils were only inches from Bella's face, taking in her scent. She could feel his energy, sense his excitement, and wondered if the horse felt her anticipation. Finally he nibbled on the carrot and she reached out to touch him, to feel his white star. She petted his nose, warmer and softer than she had imagined, and he almost pushed her off the fence with a playful nudge. Bella boldly wrapped her arms around his neck, placing her cheek against his, whispering sweet nothings to this horse of her mother's, who answered in short whinnies.

She slipped the bridle over his flickering ears and cinched it up. Bella felt his hot breath on her shoulder as she lifted the feather-light saddle from the fence and laid it across his back. He stood perfectly still, as if wanting her to mount and ride him.

Breathing hard like the horse, Bella tightened the saddle, tugging on it twice. She ran her small hand along the tender nape of his neck, and then pulled him slightly closer to the fence. The horse stood poised and ready as she eased herself up into the saddle.

For several seconds neither horse nor rider breathed or blinked.

And then they were off, moving swiftly through the shadowy night, cantering over sloping fields between wild onions and angled moon-beams. Bella's every move soon became succinct with the graceful gait of the strong, muscular animal. She could feel the stallion's power as they melded together, held motionless in mid-air as one entity. Soon the canter became a gallop, the beat of his pounding hooves even faster beneath her. They crossed the meadow in short order, with her heart beating wildly and her breath coming in short bursts. Once they came upon the upper pasture, Desperado instinctively ran a safe distance from the rim of Echo Canyon.

Bella had no control over her destiny now. She had placed it all in the will of the horse when she climbed aboard, wanting to be a part of his bold and reckless freedom. But no matter what happened she could not be sorry, because she felt more alive and closer to her mother at this moment than she had in her entire life. Bella even thought she saw her mother's smile in the shadows of the trees, and could have sworn she heard her mother's voice in the hum of the wind, cheering her on.

Suddenly wolves howled, their echoes lifting hauntingly to the upper pasture. What would the stallion do? Where would he go? The horse slowed his pace at the end of the upper field and bit at the metal latch of a heavy wooden gate until it swung free, moaning and squeaking as if reluctant to do so. It was as if he had a destination in mind, or perhaps a date with destiny.

Once outside the gate, Desperado descended a narrow sloping path to Echo Canyon below. Bella had never been in the canyon. As Nana had said, she was forbidden to ride there. Most horses spooked at the entrance, sensing danger from wolf packs that bred within the caves and hid among the boulders.

Only a wild and daring desperado would defy the odds of coming up against a wolf pack in the canyon. Bella instantly felt as much a misfit running away from her chains of reason as this brave and cunning horse. Riding on instinct and raw courage along the narrow road, the sound of clicking hooves ricocheted off sheer stone walls on either side until abruptly the stallion stopped, almost throwing Bella over his head.

Tightening her legs around the saddle she peered out into the starry night and saw four, five . . . six large silver wolves with bright amber eyes. They growled wickedly, curling back their mouths to expose pink gums and sharp teeth. Two stood before them crouched low and ready to spring, while four others perched on boulders above.

The stallion threw his head back and made a shrill sound. He stomped his front foot, hammering the powerful hoof into dry sandy soil. Sweat formed on Bella's forehead, and fear overwhelmed her. Panting and pulsing as one with the stallion, she pondered limited options until finally Desperado reared up. He stood nearly erect and pawed his front legs wildly in the air, releasing a high-pitched whinny that echoed long and slow across the narrow gully.

Bella clutched his mane and dug her heels into his belly, but began sliding off the saddle, until a sudden gust of wind burst upwards from the valley floor. She pulled herself back into place while the cold breeze blew playfully through her long hair. Were the intoxicating ride and threatening wolves affecting Bella's sensibilities, or did she smell her mother's perfume? It was one of many fading memories, but, oh so sharp and clear at this moment!

The stallion eased his legs down and held his handsome head high as the wolves suddenly relaxed. Their noses unwrinkled and the sharp teeth were no longer exposed as the canines squatted low. The cold gusty wind that had saved Bella from falling blanketed everything in icy silence. Squinting at moonlight flickering through the brushy trees, Bella thought she saw the shadowy image of a woman near the stallion's head. She had gold shimmering hair and a smooth angular face.

Had her mother come along to save her from the wolves in Echo Canyon? Come to save her from the same fate that had been her own? The wispy white presence suddenly held the reins of Desperado, petting the horse's soft white star until his breathing became slow and measured. Bella stared at the ghost of her mother, who handed the reins over with a warm smile. The wolves instantly scattered and soon could be heard at a distance, howling from atop the canyon ridge. Then suddenly the apparition of her mother disappeared.

For a fleeting second, time stopped for horse and rider. The distant howling ceased, and the night held them captive. It felt as if they were wedged between moonbeams and echoes, now and then, life and death, beginnings and endings. Finally, Desperado tossed his head, stomped his foot, and took off into the night.

He galloped through the last half-mile of Echo Canyon and across the meadow to the garden gate, where Bella dismounted the chestnut stallion. She removed her mother's English saddle and the hackamore bridle. Silently she put them back into the shed and brought out brushes for grooming. While filling a bucket with cool water for the stallion to drink, Bella stared at the moon and stars, no different really than before the ride. Yet everything seemed changed forever.

Bella petted the stallion's sweaty neck one last time, and then crept carefully back into the screened front porch. Falling exhausted into her bed, she listened to the endless hum of a million crickets. Somehow they sounded the same as always, but she was not. Bella was suddenly determined to face her father and make him see that Desperado was hers now. She knew in her heart that her mother would agree.

Early the next morning Bella looked out her window onto the meadow and watched the tall grass blow gently in the morning breeze. She could barely believe that she was sixteen, and had ridden the stallion last night on her birthday. Her heart leapt into her throat. Had her mother really saved her from falling off Desperado in Echo Canyon, protecting them both from the wolves? Or had she only imagined it all?

Bella dressed hurriedly and ran to greet her new companion. She climbed up on the white board fence and shielded her eyes from the morning sun. Whistling long and low, Bella wished she had stopped in the kitchen for a carrot. She was startled to hear her father's voice and turned to see him walking up beside her.

"Well, *Isabella*, as you have mentioned several times already, sixteen is quite grown-up." He put one arm around her, squeezing gently. "I think you need a more spirited animal now that you're a young lady."

Bella looked away from her father to the distant corner of the pasture where Desperado tossed his head, and swished his tail. The stallion pawed the earth, and then headed toward her, breaking into a handsome trot. He strolled up to the white board fence, as if on cue, and nearly knocked Bella off balance with his star-blazed nose. Desperado whinnied. Bella looked at her father, whose eyes asked for an explanation.

"I've already chosen a new horse, Father." Bella paused and felt her hands becoming damp. She forced herself to look into her father's eyes. "I want Desperado. I want my mother's horse, and Mother would want me to have him. I know she would." Bella put her arms around the stallion's neck. "Please, Father," she begged. "I feel connected to her through this horse. She loved Desperado, and so do I." Blinking back tears she waited for a response.

Her father nervously ran fingers through his graying hair and sighed. "Bella, this animal hasn't been ridden in years."

"That's not true. I rode him last night." Bella's stomach did flip-flops as she bravely confessed to her rebellious birthday ride.

"You what? Bella! There's no way that stallion would let you ride him." Her father sounded more curious than accusing.

Bella slipped one leg over the horse's back, digging her hands into his mane. Desperado whinnied softly, tossed his head, and pranced gingerly in a wide circle.

Her father folded his arms in disbelief, staring first at her, and then at the horse. "How, Bella? How did you do this? When did this happen?"

"Last night," she admitted. "It was my birthday present to me. I needed to do it, to show you that I could."

He said nothing, rendered speechless by the content of her confession.

Desperado stood still, his body poised and collected. Bella patted his velvety neck, and waited. Waited for her father to understand and believe in her rite of passage. Waited for him to let go of the child and embrace the woman emerging before him.

"Is this what Nana meant when she told me there was a surprise coming?"

Bella shrugged. "Maybe Nana saw the bond growing between Desperado and me these past few months."

"I should have known," her father replied wearily. He stared at Bella on Desperado as if not really seeing her at all, but someone else entirely."

"Okay. You win," he said in defeat. "The horse is yours." He shook his head. "But you must never ride in Echo Canyon!" he warned.

"I won't. I promise," Bella answered cheerfully as her father headed back to the house. It was a promise she could keep, because she knew there was a whole world out there for her to explore—beyond the garden gate, and even Echo Canyon. Fidgeting with the special birthday necklace, she stared at Nana in the garden puttering about the flowerpots. The old woman looked over at her and winked.

Bella winked back.

Had Nana known all along how the birthday ride would happen, and how her mother would come along to save her from the wolves in Echo Canyon? Bella had no idea. What she did know was that her mother was a kindred spirit. They both loved the stallion and lusted for adventure. Somehow she knew her mother would always be there, smiling in the shadows, cheering her on.

Birthday wishes really do come true.

betrayal

an easter eve tale of redemption

I sat at an outside table and ordered a cappuccino, watching the morning sunrise behind tall narrow shops in the *Piazza Novana*. Pigeons perched on marbled heads of carved figures in the fountain, and cooed at vendors setting up various wares. I thought about Marcella, turning eight this Easter weekend. I hadn't seen a picture of her for two years, since my sister's death. But certainly she would still look like Arianna, with those beautiful, haunting eyes.

As I strained to look for an old man and young child, I noticed instead a small scruffy dog crouching low across the cobbled Piazza. A curly-haired girl scooped up the mutt and scolded it in a high-pitched tone as she sat down and leaned against the fountain. The child folded skinny legs around the treasured pet.

Next to her an elderly man began to set up paintings. Surely this was my niece Marcella with her Grandpapa Gianni. A flock of swallows flapped noisily past and veered in their direction. They dipped down and fluttered by, as did my heart at that moment. I paid my bill for the cappuccino and crossed the Piazza, watching the old man unroll his canvases and place them on display.

"Your paintings are very nice," I said, looking into his color splashed canvases. His warm eyes studied me.

"*Grazie.* I paint for fun. An old man indulging a passion. I don't need the *euros*, just the fresh air and attention." He laughed.

"Is this your grandchild?" I looked closely at the girl, a younger version of my sister. I regretted never having visited Arianna during the last seven years of her life, cut short in such a tragic way. I could barely resist the urge to run over and gather Marcella into my arms, as the sharp pain of having lost my sister returned for the first time since her death. Why had she made the impulsive decision to marry an Italian and live in Rome?

"Yes, indeed she is my grandchild, Marcella. See?" He shuffled through the paintings and stopped when the child's portrait appeared. It took my breath away. He so perfectly captured this young girl before us on the canvas. Yet every bit of Arianna was there too, in the dark curly hair, the lean delicate frame.

"How much?"

"For you, one hundred and fifty euros."

"What if she is my niece? Then is it a gift?" After only seconds of disbelief, recognition registered on his weathered face.

"*Si*, you have a likeness to her mother."

Marcella walked over and peered up at me, the scruffy mutt bulging in her arms. "You are my aunt?"

"Yes. I am your Aunt Carissa. Your mother was my sister." I smiled at her, and knelt down to be at eye level. We stared at each other for a second, and then hugged long and hard, as if trying to fill our void of unsettled despair over the loss of Arianna.

"How incredible it is." Furrows of worry appeared on Mr. Gianni's forehead.

"Let's talk." I stood and faced the man whose son had no doubt murdered my sister. But without evidence, what crime is tried in court?

"*Si*." Marcella's grandpapa glanced at a restaurant near the plaza. "There," he pointed, "that one is mine." He shouted to the vendor set up beside him, words flowing between them like poetry set to music. An accordion player's melancholy tunes drifted over from the *Triton* fountain, and a carriage passed by, the horse's hooves clip-clopping on cobbled stones. Rome was vivid at this moment, a dizziness of sights and sounds when I met at last my little niece. Arianna's legacy!

I followed Marcella and her grandpapa to the corner café, his paintings apparently being watched by the other artist with whom he had spoken. Sitting at a table in the sun, cappuccinos magically appeared at the snap of Mr. Gianni's fingers. There was an air of distinction about him here on his established turf, not felt in the open Piazza.

"How is it you knew where to find us?" A more somber Gianni senior made a sweeping gesture to the fountains, vendors, and shops of Piazza Novana.

"When you shipped me Arianna's things, there was a painting—a rolled canvas. It was of my sister." I took a sip of the cappuccino, not sure how to continue.

"*Si.* I paint the beautiful girl, my daughter-in-law. It is sad that she is gone." The softness in his tone gave me courage to continue.

"A letter had been stashed in the rolled up painting. It was Arianna's handwriting, and her words were quite desperate. Perhaps they were her last."

Marcella sat quietly and sipped on lemonade. Her scruffy friend had been whisked away to the back of the café and promised scraps of meat by one of her grandpapa's waiters. The dog's exact whereabouts did not seem worrisome to her. I hesitated to go on. The child's resemblance to Arianna caused tears to pool in my eyes, shaded by dark glasses.

"Marcella, go help Antonio feed scraps to your little pet," Mr. Gianni cajoled. The child nodded and scooted off her chair. She smiled up at me and then skipped away.

"A letter? From Arianna?" Mr. Gianni appeared anxious.

"Yes." I leaned forward and spoke softly. "She implied that her life was in grave danger."

"What kind of danger?"

"Your son, who had charmed my sister at first, soon began to display a bad temper, and tried to control her every move. Arianna goes on in the letter to say how he was often unreasonable, leaving her alone for long periods of time, not allowing her activities outside the home."

My words fell heavy between us as the old man slowly nodded.

"Mr. Gianni, Arianna was a complicated person—young, impulsive, always looking for something more. She came to Rome as an eighteenth birthday present, and never returned for university in the fall."

"Yes. She was a restless one, and too independent for my Raphael. I tried to warn him. He would not listen." He set his jaw as sadness overcame him. "Arianna, frightened and lonely, eventually had an affair with a street artist. Raphael found out. He was livid, threatening to never let her leave his sight again, not to see her lover, or to visit America with their daughter." He shook his head slowly. "Arianna took her life soon after, so troubled was she by his transformation into a jealous, angry husband . . . and then there was her isolation, and no possible way to return to the homeland she dearly missed."

"Was the poisoned vino that my sister drank by choice?" I stared into the old man's eyes, but he quickly looked away. "I think not. She felt her life in danger according to the letter, and she had a child to care for."

Pulling the letter from my purse I held it crumbled in my sweaty palm for him to examine, but he didn't take it, only glancing at the wadded pages. "I knew Arianna better than anyone. My sister would never abandon her little girl, no matter the amount of her misery."

"What do you want from me? From this visit?" he asked, while staring at the fountain.

"Marcella."

He looked me full in the face and I could almost see the words stab his heart.

"I thought this day might come." His eyes were swimming with grief.

"I have no family, sir, except for the child. My sister and I lost our parents in an untimely accident just prior to Arianna's adventure in your Eternal City. My niece is all that I have, and she is not your grandchild. It grieves me to tell you this, but Marcella is not a Gianni. Her father is the young man you speak of who paints in the Piazza."

The proud man sighed deeply. "I can forgive Raphael many things, but not the death of Marcella's mother. I believed Arianna took her life because of the misery he inflicted upon her." He beat his withered fist on the cloth-covered table. "But to think he might have killed her, and now you are ripping Marcella from my life because he is not the father, this I can never forgive! Perhaps her blood does not run in my veins, but her love fills up my heart."

We were both silent, as if the weight and power of what defines family fell squarely between us.

After a torturous silence Mr. Gianni spoke. "You will not reveal this incriminating letter to anyone of authority if I let the child go?"

I assured him I would not.

He disappeared into the apartment above the restaurant and returned with Marcella's passport and birth papers.

"My son, he brings much disappointment to me, but he is still my son. I will not try and stop you, but you must hurry before he finds out about your plan."

I stood to leave and stared at this man who loved my sister's child as if his own. I wanted to hug him despite our divided interests, but we were nonetheless adversaries. Instead I rushed to the kitchen and wasted no time convincing Marcella to gather up the beloved mutt and come with me to America, where her grandpapa could have a nice long visit as soon as she was settled in.

"I will live with you?" Marcella asked.

"Yes, darling . . . in America. Where your mama grew up. She would want that for you."

"Will I see Papa again?" Marcella asked.

"Of course. He can visit you too." I felt a wave of anxiety and wondered how and when to tell her the truth about her mama and her two papas, both her real father and her mother's murderer.

"When will I see them? How soon can Papa and Grandpapa visit?"

"I'm not sure, sweetie." I mustered my best reassuring smile.

"Wait," Mr. Gianni pleaded, standing in the doorway.

"What?" I nearly shouted.

"I have something . . . your sister's journal. I forgot to put it in the trunk, because it was here, where she liked to sip on her cappuccino . . . and write . . . into the wee hours of the night."

He disappeared from the arched doorway of the kitchen. Marcella stood beside me and petted the ragged canine spilling over in her tiny arms while we waited. When the old man returned he placed a small leather-bound book in my hands. I tossed it into my purse.

Mr. Gianni kneeled down to hug Marcella while the tiny dog squirmed between them. Bells chimed at the cathedral nearby as we left hand in hand. My niece looked back for a final glimpse of her grand-papa and I glanced at the surrounding cafés with their outdoor tables and carefree patrons. No one seemed the wiser for my taking of the child or my breaking of the old man's heart on this Saturday before Easter.

Safely aboard the plane and with Marcella soon asleep beside me, I pried the lock off the journal and read my sister's pages and pages of neatly scripted longhand. She spoke of her jealous husband who left her alone for many days and of finding evidence he was unfaithful whenever he traveled with his work. Then she wrote about how she had taken up painting to pass the time, and how she fell in love with an artist who displayed his work in the Piazza. My sister wrote about Raphael's volatile anger once he learned of her love for the artist. She suspected that her husband had paid someone to follow her.

When I reached the middle of the journal, tucked there in the crease were two plane tickets for America—one for Marcella, and the other for Arianna. She planned to return home, probably in secret, and on the day after her death. Why would she commit suicide the day before her return home? I wept tears of sorrow for her failed attempt to escape the man who in the end derailed her plans, as well as her life.

A few weeks later I could not believe what I read in an article on the second page of the Rome Sunday paper, which was routinely delivered to my door, albeit a week late. It said Mr. Gianni's son, Raphael, was found dead Easter morning after he drank a bottle of poisoned vino. Upon interviewing neighbors and friends, it was made clear how the poisoned wine was kept to saturate crumbs left for rats in the kitchen, and coincidentally was drunk on one other occasion two years ago by Raphael's wife, Arianna Gianni. Police never established whether that, too, was a tragic accident, or a successful suicide.

Was Raphael's death as much a murder as Arianna's had been? Was it Mr. Gianni's final revenge upon his son for the loss of Marcella, not even his grandchild to begin with? Perhaps that was the last straw for the old man, his son's betrayal of everything dear to him . . . honor and heritage. Or perhaps, Raphael took his own life, upon the realization that he'd lost everything . . . including his father's respect.

I glanced at Marcella, seated across from me, nibbling toast while laughing at American cartoons on the TV. Her scruffy little friend lay at her feet, his tail wagging contentedly.

I smiled at them through tears of joy . . . from having my niece home with me at long last. Marcella glanced up at me. "Why are you crying, Aunty Carissa?" she asked.

"No reason, really. I am just so happy to have you here," I confessed, and as the child's face broke into a wide grin, it was Arianna I saw smiling back at me through those beautiful, haunting eyes.

silent whispers

i fear the days
those shards of time
when you are gone
and my mind whispers
in the hollows
of love lost and
plays its game
to silence the flames
those sustaining fires
that free my soul
and lift it on wings
of hope, desire
anticipation
i dread the day
when my love
that rushes
as a river running
within my veins
can no longer flow
from me to you
to warm your soul
and mine

half moon cay

We disembarked from the tender of the MS Rotterdam to the sound of strumming guitars. Every note clung to the breeze and drifted toward the pier. Translucent turquoise swells spilled upon powder-white sand of a moon-shaped shore and held time hostage like a revolving door with no exit.

I followed the music to its source, where open-air shops sold puka shell necklaces and bamboo flutes. It was there I joined other cruise patrons who sat beneath umbrellas sipping iced drinks through long straws. Closing my eyes I listened to lively tunes played on fast-moving strings. The trio of musicians meandered among tourists, who were bantering with shopkeepers in the trinket-filled tents, giving a festive voice to the midmorning.

Inhaling salty breezes I let my mind absorb the sights, sounds, and flavors of this tiny postcard paradise which held us somewhere between the rainforests of Costa Rica and our final destination of Ft. Lauderdale, where we would return to lives put on hold.

The sun warmed my skin like hot exotic oil as I sat beside one of many tables clustered near the center of the plaza. Periodically fellow writers from aboard ship would collapse in cushioned chairs nearby to talk with me, not considering I might be sleeping beneath my shaded eyes and quiet body. They began their conversations midstream, our consciousness attuned by now to one another and the work of our journey . . . writing stories for an anthology about the Caribbean.

It had been a surreal experience filled with more imagery than a writer could invent. Travel brochures and geography books could not give justice to the vivid mixture of island cultures, combined with the wonders of nature unfolding before us in the last ten days. I would need months to process all of it, just as it had taken months to process the reality of my loss. November eighth is when Trent left me. Four months and four days before setting foot on this crescent island of Half Moon Cay. It was an experience we had planned to share. We were to celebrate his successful surgery, a full recovery. Now, instead of embracing our future, I was left to mourn his death.

It is true that from the beginning I was clear about his illness. He had told me in a plaza, not dissimilar to this one, of the heavy burden he carried, and of needing to make decisions that could not be unmade later. I will never forget it. We were at a writing retreat in Santorini, Greece. It had been another barrage of insightful sensory input. The two years between these trips were the only time together we would ever know.

Why did I allow myself to fall in love with a dying man? I ask this every day, as if we choose whom we will love rather than love choosing us. I had refused to look at the cup half empty, at the reality of our situation. There was, after all, a fifty-fifty chance the tumor could be successfully removed. Consulting doctors agreed if all went well during the tedious operation, a full recovery could be expected, regardless of predicted complications. However, until the patient was lying unconscious and split open beneath intense surgical lights, it was anyone's guess.

Being an optimist and a dreamer, I wanted to believe that nothing would go wrong. I wasn't listening when the doctors spoke of a worst-case scenario. I refused to hear those two little words: *high stakes.* Although I didn't realize it at the time, those high stakes were mine as much as Trent's, and I am the one left to live with the hurt, anguish, and loss. I am the one left behind bleeding, empty, and raw from a surgery I did not have. Damaged and in need of recovery from scalpels that never touched me, yet with no one to blame but myself for having loved him, and oddly, with no regrets.

These, ironically, were almost Trent's exact same words when opting for the risky surgery to buy more time . . . *no one to blame but myself for having loved you, and no regrets.*

I abandoned the open plaza filled with cruise patrons and fellow writers, taking a path to the beach densely lined with shiny broad-leafed foliage. It stretched far around the half moon curve. My feet found their way to the tide line where gentle waves rushed near and splashed about my ankles. I recalled the last time I walked on a beach, and almost felt Trent beside me once again. Our silent worries about his upcoming surgery couldn't shadow the joy in our hearts for each other. What is hope if not believing in happy endings?

I watched my young friend Kyla dig fingers into damp sand and carve a moat around her castle. Blonde hair wet from splashing in the sea clung to her freckled face.

"Hi Krista!" She squinted up at me with eyes bluer than the shimmering surf.

"Hi to you too," I said, smiling back.

We had bonded aboard ship the first night. It was our third time around the dessert buffet. Obviously, we shared a similar insatiable desire for chocolate-covered strawberries. Soon we were laughing about how our names, as well as tastes, were quite similar.

I kneeled in the sand and admired her labor of love. For an eight-year-old, Kyla had more fortitude than many adults I knew. Her castle was three-tiered, with admirable detail considering the limitation of her tools. A soft-drink straw, broken shell, and smooth round stick were all she had to work with. It made me realize how much of the magic is in the artist's imagination.

A wave spilled over and crept into the moat. We watched it recede, the trapped water sinking into the sand.

"Why doesn't the moat stay full?" Kyla asked.

"Because the bottom is porous, not solid like cement."

"I know a Bible song about shifting sand," Kyla confided. She lay back, disappointed in her empty moat, and stared into the sky.

"So do I. It says to build your house upon the rock."

"Is that so the moat will hold water?"

"In a way," I replied.

Lying back in the cool, damp sand beside her, I noticed white clouds in odd shapes that had escaped my attention before now. The hungry tide licked at the castle near our feet as we silently viewed cotton sculptures in the blue beyond.

"Are you one of those writers on the ship?" Kyla asked, knowing nothing about me beyond my love of strawberries dipped in dark-chocolate.

"Yes I am."

"How many stories did you write?"

"Three."

"I like stories. What are they about?"

I didn't answer right away, realizing I hadn't considered the theme of my work until that moment. "Death. Cancer. Having one's life change direction midstream."

"Sad stories?"

"I guess so."

We watched the clouds form new shapes and listened to voices on the beach chairs behind us. Occasionally someone laughed. "Why?" my little friend inquired.

Again I had to force a response, my throat suddenly dry, my breathing quicker. "Because I recently lost someone very important to me." I heard the soft whooshing sound of the tide as a wave of emotion rushed over me. I could almost hear Kyla thinking as she stared at puffy white floating sculptures.

"I remember when Grandpa died last summer. I miss him."

I tried to focus on the clouds and not how much I missed Trent. I couldn't form the words to tell her that I knew what she meant.

"He used to read me stories, and he was never cross with me," Kyla shared.

I realized for the first time that Trent had never been cross with me either, but I could not express this, the words frozen within me.

"Look! See the castle?" Kyla pointed to a certain cloud.

I swallowed hard and took a long breath of humid air. "I see it. The one beside it looks a little like a castle, too."

"How funny!" Kyla didn't laugh. "Who do you think lives in those castles in the sky?"

"Maybe they hold dreams."

"Maybe. What dream would you put in your castle?"

"I don't know, how about you?"

"I want one of my friend Jenna's kittens."

"That's a nice dream." I wished something so simple could bring me pleasure. Maybe that was the dream to put in my castle, being able to experience joy again without a stabbing pain in my heart to compete with it.

We watched the clouds silently until they dispersed. I left Kyla busy shoring up her art sculpture, now lopsided on the tide line.

Walking past the last sunbather along the curved shore I read a sign that said *no lifeguard beyond this point*. I wished for a sign that read *no pain beyond this point*. One did not appear. I sat on the warm shifting sand, staring into the horizon where turquoise sea met cyan sky, and cried until they merged as one.

This day on Half Moon Cay blended the beginning and ending of my Caribbean journey like watercolors on canvas. Grief, anger, and despair suddenly spilled out like tubes of paint, one hue bleeding into the next, giving a softer edge and multiple dimensions to the painting of my life. Joyful memories blurred the sobriety of death, making a bittersweet canvas I would not alter one stroke of.

Had Kyla's work of art washed completely away yet? I thought about how anything not built on solid ground might succumb to the tide's ebb and flow.

It doesn't stop any of us from building sandcastles.

The ship blew its warning whistle for the last ride back in the tender to the Rotterdam, waiting to return me home. I was ready to disembark in the morning on the mainland, and resume my busy life that left no time for reflection, especially about things that might have been.

It was time to embrace things still meant to be.

the burial

pumpkin's plight

I pulled up to the Woodman home on an overcast Oregon morning, excited to spend the weekend taking care of my four granddaughters. Their parents had escaped to the coast for the annual wine tasting festival, and this was my annual alone time with those precious blonde beauties!

Shouting, "Where is everyone?" as I entered the front door caused a tangle of little girls to come running down the stairs. Hailey, the oldest at twelve, handed me a note with all the day's activities on it.

After helping me unpack, the girls ran outside to play. I peeked into Hailey and Taryn's room with Canyon, the family's faithful Golden Retriever right behind me. Where was Pumpkin? The hamster's cage was missing. I turned off Taryn's laptop, after reading a couple lines of her latest story staring at me from the screen. At only ten, Taryn was quite the inspired writer.

Stepping into kindergartner Paityn's room I straightened stuffed animals sprawled across her bed while glancing at my watch. It was time to leave for Maya's basketball game. Third in the lineup of Woodman girls, Maya was distinctly known as the tomboy of the family.

Throughout the game I watched her run from one end of the court to the other at full speed, while her sisters cheered loudly. We celebrated an easy win by ordering shakes at a carryout window.

The younger girls decided to ride their bikes when we returned home, but Hailey was doing schoolwork. I sat beside her on the bed and asked, "Where's Pumpkin?"

"Pumpkin?" Hailey's eyes glazed over. "Well, she's gone."

"Gone?" I waited for an explanation.

"Yeah. Pumpkin got out of her cage when the door didn't latch. We found her a week later, belly up in a pile of laundry."

"I am so sorry, Hailey," I said apologetically, gently pushing hair off her shoulder and looking into her eyes. "Did you have a proper burial for her?"

"Not yet."

"Not yet?"

We stared at each other and Hailey shrugged.

"Pumpkin is in the freezer."

"The freezer? You mean, next to the ice cream?"

Hailey's eyes were tearing up. I pulled her close for a tight hug and asked, "Why is Pumpkin in the freezer?"

"We haven't had time to bury her."

"How sad," I replied. "No time for a funeral."

"I've never been to a . . . funeral. What do you do at one?" Hailey asked.

"A funeral is when you put the deceased in the ground, and say a few nice things about them. Maybe add a prayer and sing a hymn."

Hailey nodded as she thought about that. "Can we have a funeral for Pumpkin today?"

"Sure. Why not? We can do it right after your dance performance. Maybe Taryn can write a eulogy and Maya can dig the hole," I suggested.

"What can I do?"

"You can find the perfect song to play, and prepare a proper casket."

"Okay." Hailey smiled. "What about Paityn?"

"She can pick flowers. I saw some blooming along the back fence."

It was settled. Hailey told her siblings before changing into warm-ups for the dance competition. My oldest granddaughter didn't miss a beat during her performance. Driving home the girls collaborated on their funeral assignments. I began dinner while Taryn wrote Pumpkin's eulogy at the table. From the window I could see Paityn picking flowers for the basket we'd found. Maya was in the garden digging a hole and Hailey was in her room decorating a shoebox.

Paityn bounced in the door with her dutifully stuffed flower basket just as I drained the macaroni. Taryn announced her eulogy was finished, and while washing her hands at the sink, Maya confirmed that the grave had been dug.

"Somebody call Hailey," I said, not looking up as I poured cheese sauce on the pasta and mixed it all together.

"I'll get her," Maya offered, always ready for action.

Paityn buttered the baking dish, I added the cheesy mac, and Taryn sprinkled bread crumbs on top while we waited for Hailey. She finally appeared with her decorated shoebox as I placed the casserole in the oven.

Somberly, I removed the hamster from the freezer. Pumpkin looked rather peaceful in her Ziploc bag as I laid her in the glitter-covered casket. Hailey grabbed the CD player, Taryn clutched her eulogy paper, Paityn held the basket of flowers, and Maya led the way to the gravesite.

We stood in a semicircle at the head of the garden just as the sun began to set behind us. The clouds had cleared enough to let streams of pink and orange seep through.

I sat the shoebox on the ground near the grave. Hailey played her CD preset at a teenage love song about never forgetting someone who was no longer there. When it had finished I nodded at Taryn, who cleared her throat.

"We are gathered here today to say goodbye to our friend, and Hailey's pet, Pumpkin. We all loved her very much." Taryn's voice broke and Paityn began to cry. Taryn pulled herself together and continued. "We'll miss Pumpkin, but when we see her grave we'll always remember how she used to sit on our shoulders and sometimes nibble our fingers."

Everyone took a moment to chuckle quietly, and Paityn laughed right out loud. It brought a smile to Hailey's otherwise gloomy face.

Head bent respectfully, Taryn folded her hands with the eulogy paper crumpled between them. Everyone looked at the ground when she began to pray. "Dear God, thank you for letting us have Pumpkin, even if it was just for a little while. Please protect her grave from our dog, Canyon, who loves to dig. Amen."

I nodded at Maya, who carefully placed the box in her well-dug hole, unable to keep from grinning when she realized it was the perfect size. Hailey looked at me and I nodded, so she picked up a handful of loose dirt from the pile beside the hole and tossed it onto the shoebox. Then she pulled a purple jonquil from Paityn's basket and laid it on top.

The ceremony was over, the sun was set, and the chill in the air grew quickly as we began singing the chosen hymn "Jesus Loves Me." Everyone helped fill the hole with loose dirt. When finished, we took turns stomping our feet on top to secure the gravesite.

"I have a surprise!" Maya pulled a cross out of her coat pocket, made by tying two sticks together with fishing line. She handed it to Hailey, who stuck it into the soft earth at the front of the grave. In the near darkness, we all took a moment to admire it.

Arm in arm we returned to the house, now filled with the scent of macaroni and cheese baking in the oven. The girls bubbled over with comments all through dinner about the ceremony. It was as if a cloud had been lifted by putting Pumpkin in her final resting place.

"Wow, I thought that hole you dug was going to be too big," Taryn told Maya.

"Me too," she agreed. "But then the box fit just right," Maya added triumphantly.

"My flowers were really pretty, huh, Hailey?" Paityn looked at her big sister.

"Yes they were, Paityn. They were beautiful."

Hailey smiled and the room lit up.

I wondered if the hamster had thawed out yet, and I was grateful the warmth of her funeral would live in Hailey's heart forever.

fancy

the ghost of art

I live in the shadows of the art academy. Come and go at my leisure. Like a gust of wind I enter the stuffy classrooms and shuffle through oversized books on the great masters. I rummage through stacks of unfinished student art, born in a momentary frenzy of creative thought and then tossed aside when falling short of the vision.

No one sees me enter or leave. Sometimes heads turn when I breeze past sweaty faces in the painfully warm classrooms, harboring half-decayed crickets in dusty corners. Day after weary day I watch youthful energy pour onto pages in spiral sketchpads. Charcoal swirls in the air and leaves a gray mist that settles on the desks.

In the dead of night when students have long gone home to sleep I contemplate the soft glow of their creative energy, still hovering over each chair. It always stuns me, as I watch, mystified. If I sit in one of the seats a warmth tingles through my being and these fingers, ghastly white as death, itch to hold drawing pencil or pen one more time . . . just once more.

I must confess it is what keeps me rooted to this world, and equally prevents my leaving. That energy . . . that spark of creative musing flitting about and never landing, never burning out, not able to be snuffed like a spent candle.

I don't hold the secret to life, but certainly, I can mold it. Just as I might mold clay or carve marble into breathtaking thought-provoking art. Since what feels like forever I have labored over this or that treasured piece of work in those silent hours where the forsaken play. Even knowing that every coveted line of perfection will fade with morning light. Vanish completely, leaving once again a blank page.

This is when I become riled, like a suitor having caught his cherished lover with another. I begin to pace these high-ceilinged halls of my hallowed institute. Students still lurking about somewhere, driven to finish a piece or meet a deadline, have been known to flee witlessly at the hollow echo of my feet on the oak stairwell. All too often, I must confess, I run dizzily throughout the cathedral-size structure, intensely distraught over the injustice of it all.

Yet every new day at just past midnight I begin my glorious physical expulsion onto pristine white paper or canvas with affectionate stroking of pencil or brush. I might choose sharp lines or rich hues, whatever my devilish delight. Such a release of emotion it allows, no, demands! My thoughts blur with anticipation while hands shake and eyes tear at the thought of caressing each and every inch of canvas. An explosion of all that I am and was, and can yet become.

The intimacy alarms me, shocks me even now, after all these years of painstakingly creating on canvas or sketchpad two dimensional realities, exposing every aspect of them in naked, three dimensional truth. New truth. Gut-wrenching truth. Staring at me in the intoxicatingly rich oils, or dark dusty charcoals. Sometimes for a twist, I create in powerful pastels, so flirtatious and bold. Sharp wet ink, shaded pencil line. Whatever the medium, all seduce, console, and gently soothe my fired-up, frantic mental state as the picture or painting magically transforms into beautiful bright shapes or images. Well, sometimes they are a little on the dark side, but then, so am I.

No matter really, for by the time dawn arrives, my masterpieces have faded beyond redemption. This agony has often nearly defeated me, made me groan with eerie wails that rattle the heavy-framed paintings on the thickly plastered walls. It is legend, my heartfelt frustrations crying out through the classrooms. Many refuse to enter the premises for fear they might meet the crazy spirit of this art institute. This is how they refer to me, as a crazy spirit. So unfair. For I have not assaulted them in any way, not touched a hair on their young thickly-maned heads.

Quite the contrary, I enhance their visual perception. You might say

I *am* their visual perception. For it is I who breathes life into their naïve thoughts, their nearly completed notions needing a push up and over the creative fence, so to speak. I woo them carefully, watch them mindfully, choose them discreetly. Only the best, of course. The most determined, most obsessed, most like me for complete and utter betrayal of reasonable thinking will do. Yes I know reason is our guide, but fancy— *fancy is what reason feasts upon when scrambling to a higher level.*

Once I have carefully chosen my prey, I instill a vision. Of what, you ask? Well, of my beloved vanished masterpieces of course! My slow steady gust of genius plays with the ends of their hair and widens their youthful pupils. Lustfully they stare at the blank page until attacking it with all the gusto they never knew prior. No, timid and precise were their lines before my spirit seized them, wreaking havoc on their orderly, exacting methods.

And then, perhaps as few as twelve hours later, their finished piece lies before them, glistening wet on the easel. Unless of course it is done in pastels or pen or graphite, charcoal or even clay. There are no boundaries to my mediums. Or my conscience. It merely amuses me to control their delicate youthful fingers and natural gift for expressing emotion in visible form. After all, they do ultimately become renowned thanks to my influence in their work.

They are the vessel of my genius. I am the anointed one who opens their shaded eyes. You might say I gently bridge the gap, even occasionally shove them roughly into territory not yet chartered, where they fear to go, yet long to explore. The *art* of making *art* . . . breathing life into a piece of work that transcends it all. Elevate it from biological sex to seductive lovemaking. Cause emotion. Discover intimacy. Be drawn in, taken aback. They feel the tingle up and down their spines as they lavish their hearts onto the carefully plotted piece of work, raising the spirit of their creation above the restraints of mortality.

Those who are touched by my non-human hands might call me the angst that drives them. Others call me creative genius. What do I care? Invisible spirit *or ghost if you will*, intangible talent, guileless giftedness

. . . no matter the title, for it isn't explainable and isn't their power to command or control. It just *is*. I just *am*. And whatever I am, I am fleeting. I come and go. Never stick around to be recognized. It's a big world to color after all, even with broad strokes. As for pinning me down to extreme talent or lofty gift . . . I say . . . pish-posh! Genius? Creative energy? Damn them all! I am nothing more than madness!

That over-the-line-of-rational thinking we all hesitate to approach, and stiffen at the mere thought of extending a toe beyond. But some always do. And always will. Thank God. For the day the last of you fails to try, I will no longer exist. And what a bane of existence this all would be without me. Can you imagine a world without creativity? Without *art?* Written, sung, played, acted, chiseled, drawn, painted, however envisioned . . . not created?

The horror of a world doomed to complete and total sanity. The brain of reason with no dare-to-try coiled around it, no heart-felt craving to disassemble orderliness, no temptation to abuse normality. Fear me if you wish, when I stomp around the empty rooms in the wee hours of early morning or scream through the rafters above the silent halls, or play wistfully with your locks of hair like a breeze through the window. But hear this, without my presence there would be no betwixt and between. There would be no turmoil of creativity fighting to form, no unresolved imagination, nothing to fancy . . . but facts! So be thankful for creaking walls and howling wind, fairy dust and ominous feelings, without which, canvas will lack for color. Paper will hunger for musical notes and whimsical fiction.

If you want to fear something, fear imagination dying a mundane boring death, squished beneath the beast of conformity and rationality. Dread an ending to the dance, the embrace of shared emotion through hearing a sonnet or viewing a Monet. Dread that I might ever be stilled, leave the halls, silence the moan, numb the tingle, put down the pen. Hang on to glorious madness, and never let it cease. I am what powers the wings of truth through artistic impression.

Like faith, what you can't prove exists . . . makes all the difference!

asphalt jungle

filled with nocturnal beasts

Diablo pulled his collar up as he headed into the chilly north wind. His bones ached from the dampness. A streetlamp became visible in the distance, its yellow glow oozing through thick night air. Only the *click, click* of his boots could be heard as he approached the lamp. He leaned against it and lit a cigarette.

Pushing smoke out hard and long from that first rewarding puff, he thought about his need for a woman—perhaps young, with ivory skin and raven hair. He loved raven hair. But he wasn't that particular. He couldn't afford to be. Not many women who roamed the streets after dark were willing to talk with a man dressed all in black, from his coarse unruly hair to the tips of his pointed leather boots.

It must have been his lucky night. A prospect showed up, much to his amazement. She floated down the lonely walkway hardly visible at all, dressed in black from top to bottom just as he was. She hesitated at the streetlamp where Diablo still leaned, his cigarette nearly spent. The woman pulled her own pack of Camels from a coat pocket.

Diablo admired her long narrow form in the classy fur wrap. She resembled a sleek panther, but with short red hair to match her devilish smile, rather than the raven locks he'd hoped for.

"Mind if I bum a light?" the redhead purred in a voice that was husky and low, much like the wild feline her suave appearance suggested.

"Sure." He unzipped a leather pocket and extracted his lighter, carefully concealing the pocketknife beside it. Leaning forward he held the flame close, illuminating the white cigarette in the darkness surrounding them.

She took a long puff as he had done, a true chain smoker living from one nicotine break to the next. It somehow bonded him to the catlike woman and he almost regretted his intent.

"Where you headed?" he asked, knowing full well she would not be arriving.

"To the train station two blocks over. How about you?"

He hesitated, feeling suddenly aroused by her milky skin and bright green eyes. Diablo let his cigarette butt drop to the ground and smashed it under a boot, grinding back and forth methodically. He fingered the knife in his pocket, excitement in his groin area growing to the point of explosion. His heart began pumping wildly with anticipation. He could almost feel her warm blood on his hot skin, as he released himself inside of her . . . soon, very soon.

As he pulled his weapon out, the woman quickly pounced on him. Her speed was impressive. She let her long nails claw their way down his face, which he knew must be contorted in disbelief. Her cigarette fell silently to the pavement as Diablo hit the cold concrete beside it, with a thud. He lay beneath the woman, who had grabbed the opened knife and hissed *gotcha* . . . just as a sharp pain entered his side.

The hunter had become the prey. How amusing, he thought, while losing consciousness. It seemed appropriate that it should end this way, for turnabout is fair play. Lying there bleeding profusely he dreamt of big game cats roaming wild, where there was no asphalt and the fittest survived by their own merit, not trickery or debauchery.

The woman's heart beat against his as she lay above him, tensed and poised to strike a second time.

It was not necessary.

He took his last breath with no specific memories or regrets, only joyful release from this asphalt jungle of his life.

words like wings

is it a wonder how
words are like wings
that carry us with the wind
where only angels feel free?

and black on white
can lift the soul and let it sail
on the sapphire seas
of memories and dreams?

and those that know
can speak in silence
feeling the warmth
of a lover's embrace?

taste the passion in their kiss
and experience the wind, the
waves, the words written
on each other's hearts?

a many splendored thing

Swishing red vino in a stemmed glass, she saw him from across the room. His attractive form quickened the beat of her traitorous heart as she downed the Merlot. Catching a glimpse of his shadow hovering near, she beckoned the barmaid for a refill. He sat opposite her, revealing a fire in his eyes that nearly stopped her pulse. Not an ounce of seduction oozed from him, the lack of it seducing her brazenly.

She dropped her gaze from those smoldering eyes to his strong hands folded on the table. All of him was reflected in those hands. She longed to touch them, trace his fingers with her own, pick each one up and caress it gently . . . kissing every tip. Instead she fingered the stem of her glass, and waited, poised to sip on sin. Breathless with anticipation she watched the barmaid pour his, leaving the bottle with one raised brow and half a smile.

Nodding often and laughing freely she listened to him talk while hungrily inhaling scents from the kitchen—of bread baking, pasta boiling, a tomato sauce simmering. It was intoxicating, intuitively knowing his feelings for her. Did he realize she had feelings for him as well? She thought perhaps he did, but they didn't speak of it, being only friends and behaving as friends should behave.

His way with words was music for her mood, and, although just casual conversation, it made her blush nonetheless. That deep resonant voice warmed her with wanting. Merry tunes played on ivory keys of a worn piano enticed them to the dance floor. Sweet perfume and cigarette smoke hugged the air as they moved with the music. Carefully they touched as friends would touch, but then the music slowed and the room swayed. He caught her gently but then she dashed away, grabbing a purse and coat off a chair.

Fresh air filled her lungs as she bolted out the door and leaned against the streetlamp. Spicy aromas and laughter lingered in the crisp night air. *Could he walk her to her room?* he asked, but no reply escaped her lips as she hurried down the cobbled street. He caught up to her and stayed protectively near as they crossed the side alley together. When they approached the motel that housed her things, she looked up at the twinkling stars staring down as if to taunt her. They seemed to be dancing a dizzy waltz, weakening her resolve, as did that beautiful resonant voice inquiring if she was all right.

Slowly, hesitantly, she raised her hands and touched his face, thinking she saw a glimmer of longing in his expression. Pulling him to her, she gently kissed his lips. He lingered there for an eternal second, and then hungrily kissed her back. No denial. No hesitation. As if he had waited patiently for a very long time to seize this moment.

And now what?

Should she bring him up the steep flight of stairs beyond the entry, down the narrow hall to her cozy rented room? Or leave him hovering there while slipping delicately from his grasp, to greet her bed alone and face tomorrow sober—more the victor for her fortitude?

It was buried at the bottom of the trunk—a little black leather bound book. *Journal* was engraved across the front and when the young teenager opened the cover her heart sang with delight. Bringing the book with her, she settled into the wooden swing and gave it a gentle push. Before opening its cover the girl looked up and squinted into the sun. A warm wind tickled her face and teased the floppy straw hat on her grandmother in the garden across the yard.

Would her grandmother care that she'd found the journal in a forgotten attic box? Faded ink on yellowed paper revealed descriptions and observations of Rome, noted in the journal as the Eternal City. Most exciting to the thirteen-year-old were the pages that spoke of love, not for family and friends but for a boy! Such feelings were slowly awakening in her and she greedily inhaled the words written on thin worn pages of the past.

Entry for March 25th I have met someone who shares my love of photography. We sit at the outside cafés in the Piazza Novana and drink strong cappuccinos while discussing our equipment. I don't hear his wonderful insight into lenses. I only hear his distinctive voice that beckons me to take the most amazing pictures of my life. It is my newly racing heart that inspires me to see everything more vividly. The men and women in the fountains have come alive; their emotive faces more compelling than the beautiful marble on which they are carved. I think of loved ones back home and wish to share this magical scene, yet the part of me seeking what should not be left to chance is grateful for the distance.

Entry for March 26th Today we discover the wonderful scents and brilliant colors of Campo Di Fiore. Fruit and vegetable vendors shout in their native Italian. I delight in the busy arena of the marketplace. On this crisp March day we decide to meander down a narrow cobbled street to snap our frames of art. Our laughter echoes off the buildings and comes back to us, like a shadow of guilt clinging to my mind. I cannot help myself from wanting more and more time alone with him. We slip away from the photography group we have traveled here with to share steaming plates of fresh pasta in a small café. Before we know it, we are lingering over a bottle of wine long beyond the designated time to reunite with our fellow photographers. Sitting too close together in the back of a cab we are quiet, our heavy thoughts surrounding us like fog enveloping the city.

Entry for March 27th This morning our photography class visits the Sistine Chapel and St. Peter's Cathedral. Everywhere I look there are well-preserved erotic and religious paintings. The profound power of this art tugs at my heart and makes it ache, while stolen glances shared with my special friend overwhelm it with joy. Love is, as the song would suggest, a many splendored thing. Everywhere I look, I see in the work of the masters that love has often been savored in secret and frequently with a cost. I attribute this in part to the fact it is not a 'thing' we have control over. In the end you cannot fool your heart. It beats for whom it wishes and you are the victim of its choosing. You can accept it or rail against it, but you cannot change it.

Entry for March 28th Back in my hotel room I have looked up splendor and found it to mean a multitude of things such as magnificent, brilliant, a great brightness or luster. Is that not what love is? Love sharpens the senses, pierces the darkness and awakens our joy. How can something that brings such purpose and meaning to life also cause so much misery and trouble? At times it has proven to be a vile and bloodsucking monster, strangling all common sense and decency from people possessed by it. I sometimes think love is not a choice so much as a destiny, not a willful act so much as a fateful one, for when you find yourself in the throes of it, there is little you can do.

Entry for March 29th I held his hand in the dark tunnels of the catacombs. We stood side by side in awe of the coliseum. Everywhere we go our hearts and minds soak up the fascinating sculptures and canvases, thirsty for the meaning and purpose behind each one. The feelings we share give depth to the ecstasy and agony of historical art in this eternal city, where this 'thing' called love has drawn tears from bullies, strengthened the weak and dropped kings to their knees. I have learned that nothing is more debilitating, more coveted or more frightening, more incredible or more difficult to understand than love. It distinguishes men from beasts and makes beasts of men. It encompasses all that life is, drives the very core of our being and is indeed a many splendored thing, worth the price that we sometimes pay for it.

Entry for March 30th It is our last day in Rome together. In the morning we will begin our journey home. We sit on the Spanish Steps and stare at the monstrous billboards sporting fashion trends. No words come. The early morning chill stifles our humor. We agree to meet for dinner while taking photos of a foggy city steeped in shadows. For the last time, side by side we window shop. Finally we quit shooting our endless frames and have a stranger snap us in silly poses, albeit with some somber glances. I can think of nothing but the dinner we agreed to have later at a café in the piazza, with music and dancing. I happily anticipate our last night together and equally mourn my devious plan. I should not love this man, nor should I want him for my own if only this one night, yet I can think of nothing else.

That was the end of the journal entries!

What did her grandmother do?

The grandchild gave the porch swing a swift upward thrust with her bare toes. Observing her grandmother thinning petunia beds, the teenager daydreamed of faraway cities and falling in love. One day, she decided, she would travel the world and have a journal of her own, and maybe, she would ask her grandmother how the story ended.

Putting the book back into the attic box, she thought about how the ending didn't matter as much as the beginning and the middle. Because endings are never really the end where love is concerned. She knew that by how much her grandmother still loved her grandfather and spoke about him all the time even though he had been gone quite a while.

Gone and forgotten are not the same. Love lives on, even after death.

Maybe, she decided, that's what makes love splendid.

city of love

the magic of rome

I stared out the window of Vinni's café at the adorable mutt begging pastries off customers. He went from table to table of patrons sipping mochas in the first warm sun of early spring. Each person extended an affectionate pat or half-eaten scone, his shaggy tail swishing in gratitude.

"It's Hauser!" I emphatically called out to whoever might hear. But no one responded. There was not a lull in the crowded shop chatter. Obviously no one cared that I wrote my most important piece of advertising to date revolving around a dog serving alcoholic refreshment to its owner. I had done the photo shoot with a dog named Hauser . . . a dead ringer for the dog mooching scones out front.

"Hold my cappuccino!" I yelled at Vinni behind the pastry display.

I excused myself and pushed through the tightly knit people waiting to order. I ran out the open door and April in Rome overwhelmed me with the scent of sweet blossoms in the air. Overhead trellises of Wisteria danced in the warm breeze. Birds chirped incessantly from rooftops. Shop doors sat ajar and aromas mingled together . . . fried sausages, sweet breads, strong cappuccino. The street was alive with horns honking and brakes slamming . . . and then I spotted my furry friend. I knelt beside him.

"Hauser?"

I stared into his big brown eyes while scratching him behind the ears. But no, this was not Hauser. The one white paw gave it away. The real Hauser had four brown paws, wiry and slightly curled like the rest of him.

"Who are ya buddy?" I pondered his adorable friendly face. He responded with a warm lick on my cheek followed by a friendly bark.

"No one knows," the stranger seated at the table beside us answered. He rattled his newspaper and turned the page. "Apparently he's taken up residence here at Vinni's. Friendly little fellow, and smart too. He watches for traffic and never approaches anyone without a welcome."

"I see. Well, he looks just like a dog I knew once." I glanced through the front window of Vinni's shop and saw my steaming cappuccino on the counter. The crowd had thinned. Meanwhile the Hauser look-a-like made little love sounds in his throat and stared at me with ears bent slightly forward. I was falling in love with this stray . . . smitten at first sight. Granted, my initial rumblings of affection were rooted in memories of the real Hauser, but this near twin begging muffins was the epitome of endearing.

"I wonder if I could take him home?" I asked the man with the morning news, as if he were the final authority on stray mutts.

"Why not?" He put his paper down. "Rome is the city of love. Even for a stray dog." His words lingered in my mind while the April breeze tickled my face.

Vinni appeared and leaned in the doorway. He handed me the cappuccino and stared at my shaggy new friend. "Who is this? Your latest love interest?" He asked, laughing. Vinni loved to laugh, deep and wide . . . from the heart. He was a big man, but gentle as a spring shower.

"Very funny!" I wrinkled my nose at him and took the hot drink. We carefully observed the wiry little pastry beggar, who grinned at us with an obvious twinkle in his brown eyes.

"This Hauser . . . he looks like the little dog in the beer commercial you wrote last winter, no?"

"Yes, he certainly does. I'm taking him home with me, Vinni."

"Hmm. I guess I was right then."

"About what?"

"Love at first sight."

"Yeah. You could say that." It was the truth. I should have been so lucky as to find a man while ordering a cappuccino . . . one equally available, that I could love as instantly and completely as this little dog.

"Well, then, you'll need a few things." Vinni nodded in the direction that he wanted me to follow, and soon we were digging around in the back of Vinni's shop, where we found an old leather collar and a leash. The new Hauser (no other name would do) took to it instantly. Hauser whipped his tail excitedly and licked my ear as I stooped down to adjust it. He walked beside me all the way to my apartment as if he'd done this every day of his life.

I soon acquired all the best doggy paraphernalia that my young struggling career in advertising would permit. My first taste of success had been the beer ad with the original Hauser opening the fridge and bringing a bottle to his master, who appeared to be a couch veggie watching some sporting event on the telly.

That script had landed me this job in Rome. I had never ventured far from my Milan roots in the near quarter century of my life to date, so I was happy for the opportunity. But it was also lonely with no family near, and Mr. Right was escaping me, despite being in the City of Love.

A few weeks later I put the collar and leash on Hauser as usual and headed out the door for our run down the Spanish Steps and along the side streets lined with shops. Our love at first sight was still strong. Hauser provided an excited wiggle at the end of a dog-eat-dog day at work, and a warm body at the foot of my bed each night. What he lacked in sexual appeal or meaningful conversation he made up for in affectionate doggy snuggles and total devotion.

For now, it would have to do.

We rounded the cobblestoned corner of the nearly deserted early morning street, but on this particular day it landed us almost on top of a well-built man in a Gucci suit. I briefly saw a leather attaché case in his left hand before he fell beneath us, unintentionally mauled by a shocked Hauser and me.

I scrambled off this stranger and fought to regain my composure, vaguely aware of Hauser barking his fool head off. Soon Hauser was licking the alluringly handsome face of this man, who chuckled and said, "Hauser, buddy! Where've you been?"

I stood motionless, staring at the two of them, as if finding my lover in bed with another woman. "How did you know his name was Hauser?" I demanded in a suspicious tone." Not a single bruised body part mattered, suddenly, as I braced myself for a reality check.

"Well . . . it's his name." The good-looking stranger rose and made no attempt to brush dust from his Gucci suit. Instead, he instinctively rubbed and scratched various familiar parts of my newly adopted canine. "How did *you* know his name?" the man asked, with an element of incredulousness to his deep voice.

"Because . . . I'm the one who named him that!" I snapped, defensively.

Time throbbed away unnoticed as we stared at one another, polarized. Tiny currents inched up my back and stood every neck hair on end. It was his shameless pools of deep aquatic blue. They somehow soothed my ruffled pride as I finally said without blinking, "He looks like the Hauser in the beer commercial . . . you know, "Let your Hauser bring you a Hamden's . . ."

"Yeah . . . I know." The blue eyes beneath dark furrowed brows didn't waver, their gaze still intent upon me. ". . . for thirst quenching half time refreshment," he said emphatically, finishing the punch line I'd written.

"You named him for the beer commercial?" I broke the stare and glanced at our wiry little friend, smiling a full doggy smile.

"I did . . . actually . . . name him for the beer commercial."

"He's your dog?"

"Just a stray I picked up outside of Vinni's Café one day . . . but then he ran off and he's been gone for weeks. I'd given up on finding him."

"I wrote it."

"Wrote what?"

"The beer commercial."

"You're in advertising?"

"Yes."

"Me too. That's why I'm here so early, to see a client about a city shoot." He glanced at the building across the narrow alleyway in front of us. Traffic was picking up, and the slant of the sun was warmer. We simultaneously decided to offer up proper introductions and move from the street to the café on the corner, where we sat at the outside table still damp from morning dew.

Our vision locked again as we sat down and a tingling sensation shot up my spine. It was odd to be this affected by a perfect stranger who had adopted the same homeless pet. We each ordered a cappuccino and had a few laughs about Hauser, whom we could freely discuss without much awkwardness at all. I invited him back to my apartment, where he could clean up for his client. My heart plunged when he declined.

"Please, let me help you freshen up for your meeting," I insisted.

"No really, don't worry about it . . ."

"But it's the least I can do . . ."

"Let me buy you another cappuccino first . . ."

We looked into each other's eyes again and somehow I knew he felt time alone in my apartment without tumbling straight into the bed could be too hard to resist. I knew this because I was feeling the exact same thing. Surely he could reschedule with his client . . . in a couple months after we came up for air.

We had a second cappuccino. Hauser sat squarely between us with his big brown eyes twinkling up, first looking at me, and then his prior master. It was as if he knew about this possible merger. I almost suspected him of planning it. Surely he smelled the scent of his previous owner before we collided. Did he lead me to this angel of the gods?

Anything is possible, especially in the City of Love.

the hidden letter

jewels of truth

Rose ran barefoot through the trees, her long skirt catching on ivy wound around the fat trunks. She collapsed onto dewy earth near the creek and Wil caught up to her. Together they stared at the stars overhead.

"Do you see the Big Dipper?" Rose asked, still a little breathless.

"I do." Wil rolled over on his side and she could feel him staring at her.

"My father's going to miss me soon. I really need to get back to the house."

Wil's only response was to lean over and kiss her. Soon they were passionately entwined, heart rates soaring beyond what a game of chase could do. A shot went off and they quickly untangled, scrambling to their feet.

A gruff voice shouted from the distance, "Rose! Where are you?"

Rose looked for her father's familiar face lurking behind trees. "You have to go, Wil," Rose whispered. "Now! Before he finds you here." Her voice had an edge of fear.

"Are you going to be okay?" Wil asked.

"Yes, I'll be fine. But he'll kill you if he finds you here! Go!" She pressed her delicate hands against his hard chest. Wil swept a strand of strawberry-blonde hair back from Rose's damp face and kissed her one last time. The teenagers searched each other's eyes for a glimpse of the love they must hide until able to meet again.

And then he was off, his limber body barely heard rustling through the trees along the shore of the creek. No sooner had Wil sprinted away than Blaine Bradey appeared from behind a huge oak.

"Rose! Where is that no account boy?" he bellowed, confident that someone had been there with his daughter.

"I . . . I don't know what you mean, Father. I was just on a walk through the woods, alone." She folded her hands and looked innocently into his eyes.

"Young women don't take walks alone in the woods in El Dorado, CA, Rose. It isn't safe and you know it. Full of hooligans and rustlers, this whole area. Maybe one day it will be safe but not in 1881. You been with that no account boy from the Mackenzie Ranch. I forbid you to see that boy ever again, Rose. Do you hear me? I simply forbid it!" Her father's face appeared ominous in the glow of the moon.

"Why Father?" Rose asked angrily.

Blaine Bradey hesitated briefly. "Because, Rose, the boy's father, William Mackenzie . . ." his voice faltered as he awkwardly fingered his gun.

"What about his father?" Rose asked, annoyed with his constant intrusion into her personal life. She was, after all, seventeen. Plenty old enough to be treated as an adult.

"His father killed your mother!" Blaine shouted hoarsely.

Father and daughter glared at each other for a tortured second.

"I don't believe you," Rose responded flatly.

"It's the truth, Rose. I swear to God." Blaine snarled, his body contorting with rage. "The son-of-a-bitch got wasted one night and tried to rape your mother. I found them behind the dance hall in town."

He moved closer to Rose and she backed a step away.

"It was a charity ball. Everyone was there. Even that no account Mackenzie family with their dirty money made on whiskey and gambling." He punched his words out with bitter hatred and wiped his sweaty brow.

"I saw your boyfriend Wil's father leave the dance that night, and I didn't see your mother anywhere. I searched around outside and when I checked in the barn behind the dance hall . . . there he was . . . on top of her . . . mauling at her clothing."

Rose stood frozen against a tree she'd backed into. She didn't believe what she was hearing.

"I took aim at him with my pistol and then . . ." Rose's father hesitated. "Everything went dark. Mackenzie must have knocked me out. When I woke up . . . Ann Marie was dead. He'd put a knife through her heart. But the bastard was never locked up. The crooked no account sheriff owed his family lots of money for gambling debts, so he called it an accident."

Blaine's eyes became pensive slits. "Can you believe that? Put a knife right through her heart and walked away a free man."

Rose stared at him, shocked and confused. Then she turned and fled toward the house, making her way instinctively through the trees with tears blurring the cluttered path. Without a wasted second the tall willowy teenager packed her small suitcase used every summer for visiting Uncle Jake in Reno. She couldn't stay here another minute. The haunting tale of her mother's mysterious death was suffocating.

She wondered if her father's version of the tale was true, or merely a half-truth told by an embittered hate-filled man. Uncle Jake would know. He knew everything. He would tell her what had really happened that night long ago, when she became motherless while still an infant.

Rose spied the jeweled box on her dresser and dropped it into the shoulder bag. The box and its contents were her mother's, and her grandmother's. It would be hers now, the last coveted pieces of them she would ever possess.

Rose stole out the back door and with expertise swiftly saddled her horse. She took off into the starlit night with not so much as a backward glance. Once at the train station Rose bought a ticket from the night teller, guardedly producing one precious bill at a time to pay him. Despite her father's wealth, she had only a small amount of cash on hand to get her all the way to Uncle Jake's. After purchasing her ticket, she hugged the long silky neck of her chestnut mare and sent the animal off into the night, knowing it would return home.

Rose climbed aboard the train and hoped no one would suspect she was a rebellious teenager fleeing her father's house. She settled into a seat and stared blankly at the dark night out her window. *All Aboard* echoed down the tracks and a whistle punctured the air, just as a man dressed in black sat down in the seat beside her. The train pulled away from the station and Rose twirled a lock of strawberry hair around her long slender finger.

"Going far?" he asked pleasantly.

"Just to Reno," Rose replied. "What about you?"

"It's my usual trip to Boise . . . to see clients." He tipped his hat. "My name's Devin Foster."

Rose tucked unruly curls behind an ear. "I'm Rose Bradey." She could feel her cheeks become warm. "I'm going to visit my Uncle Jake."

Devin eyed her with a look of concern. "It's odd that you'd go this time of night. A young woman all alone."

Rose glanced out into the darkness beyond her window again. "I . . . I had to leave quickly." She stared at the mysterious man in black, wondering what it was he saw clients about. "My father and I had a terrible fight."

"I see." Devin rubbed his chin, as if wondering what to say. "I'm sorry. It must be scary, traveling alone without an escort."

Rose leaned back into the hard leather seat. "Do you live in El Dorado?"

"All my life."

"Me too. My father's name is Blaine Bradey. Have you heard of him?"

"Of course I have. El Dorado is too small to not know who Blaine Bradey is."

"Well, do you also know that a man named William Mackenzie killed my mother when I was just a baby?" Rose couldn't believe she'd confessed to this stranger, but somehow it had all just poured out. Maybe to help it sink in.

Devin nodded his head. "It's a fairly famous El Dorado legend."

"Father always said she'd died tragically, but he never wanted to discuss it." Rose lowered her voice as several more people entered the car and looked for a seat. "Uncle Jake told me she'd been accidentally stabbed during a fight between two men." A tear escaped down Rose's cheek and she brushed it away. "I only found out tonight that William Mackenzie was involved. And he just happens to be the father of my boyfriend, Wil." Rose lost her composure and began to sob, rummaging in her bag for a hanky.

Devin reached for a crumpled handkerchief in his shirt pocket and she took it gratefully. "As I recall," Devin admitted, "my big sister Molly and her girlfriends fussed about that tragic event for some time." Devin slid down into his seat a little and tugged on the brim of his hat. "My sister Molly was your father's age."

Rose tried to quit sniffling. "What did your sister and her friends say?"

Devin thought for a minute. "They said your mother . . . Ann Marie?"

"Yes . . . Ann Marie."

"Well, they said she was in love with that Mackenzie."

"She was in love with the man that killed her?"

"According to my sister, Ann Marie and William saw each other secretly for some time before she married Blaine Bradey. As the story goes, your mother's family didn't feel the Mackenzies were the right sort of people to marry into. Running saloons and illegal gambling establishments from here to St. Louis and all."

"What else did Molly and her friends say?"

"Well, I believe they said your mother ended up in the barn behind the dance hall one night with Mackenzie and your father, after a charity ball. Your father fought with Mackenzie and somehow your mother was stabbed. Mackenzie was acquitted, so the authorities must have believed it was an accident."

Devin slouched even further in his seat and pulled his hat over his face. "Rose, it all happened so long ago. Forget about it. What your parents did shouldn't affect you now that you're grown."

The conductor walked by and checked their tickets. Rose produced hers, moist and wrinkled, from her knotted fist. Once the conductor had moved on Devin added, "You're young and got your whole life to live. Go see your uncle and cool off for a while. Then do as you please, regardless of the past." He adjusted his hat a little to keep out the eerie glow of the oil lamps. "Don't let their ghosts haunt your closet." That was the last bit of wisdom from the man in black, who was breathing heavily, as if asleep.

What really happened that night in the barn? Surely William Mackenzie wouldn't have raped the woman he loved. Perhaps her father caught them making love. Could they have been having an affair? Unable to sleep, Rose began taking inventory of her overstuffed bag and what bare essentials she had ended up with besides the small suitcase of clothing under her seat.

She lost interest in whatever else the bag held and pulled out the jeweled box. Rose lifted the lid and admired the special lockets and delicate cameos that had captured the hearts of her dear mother and grandmother. Placing a large cameo brooch back into the box, Rose gasped as a false bottom fell away from the jeweled box and a hidden letter fell onto her lap.

She peered over at Devin, asleep beneath his hat. Rose felt satisfied that she was alone with her treasure. She unfolded the delicate paper several times and angled it slightly toward the dim light as she read:

Dear William,

I am writing you this letter to let you know how sorry I am for not standing up to my parents. I should have told them I couldn't possibly marry Blaine, and then run into your loving arms. I feel the need to tell you that Rose is your daughter. She has your smile and your eyes, and every time I look into her tiny face, I long for you.

Please try and understand how I had no choice but to marry Blaine. I have never let him touch me except on our wedding night so that he would believe he is the father of our baby. I could not allow our daughter to be looked down upon, my dearest William, and pay the price of shame for our forbidden love.

Rose stared with disbelief at the first page of the letter. William Mackenzie was her father . . . Wil's father was her father, too. How could that be? How could she have fallen in love with her own brother? What a cruel and devastating truth to bear. Her hands shaking, she turned the paper over and finished reading:

Blaine is a God-fearing man who works hard and provides well for his family. Our little Rose will never want for anything. I have heard that you and Jessica adopted her sister's baby boy after she died in childbirth. You will make a great father, William.

All My Love Forever
Ann Marie

Rose reread the part about Wil being adopted. *Thank God* she whispered into the stale air of the train car. He was not her brother!

Did Blaine Bradey find out he wasn't her real father? Did William Mackenzie find out *he was?* She wondered if her mother's death could really have been an accident, and hoped Uncle Jake knew the truth about what happened that night.

Riding up the dirt road the next morning on a horse rented from the livery stable, Rose was pleased to see a familiar face. Uncle Jake quit pounding on the new fence post. An expression of surprise mixed with confusion spread across his ruggedly handsome features.

"Rose. Did someone forget to tell me you were coming?" Uncle Jake asked, his surprise melting into joy at the sight of her.

"No, Uncle Jake. I've left home. Father and I had a terrible fight." Rose held back tears and tried to look more together than she felt.

"So your father doesn't know where you are?" Uncle Jake tried to hide his concern, but Rose saw the worry in his furrowed brow.

"I don't want him to know. Promise you won't tell, Uncle Jake." She pushed disheveled curls off her shoulder. "Father will just come for me. And I won't go with him. I'm never going back to El Dorado."

Uncle Jake lifted his Stetson to reveal hair speckled with gray. He scratched his head. "What did you and your daddy fight about, honey?"

Rose looked off into the Nevada sky as the horse tossed its head and whinnied low. "Wil. Father won't let me see him." She glanced at Uncle Jake, who leaned on the new section of fence. "His father is William Mackenzie," she added.

Uncle Jake sighed. He tugged on the rim of his hat and studied the dirt. "Your father has good reason to feel hostile toward the Mackenzies."

"What happened to my mother, Uncle Jake?" A tear escaped down Rose's cheek.

A somber Uncle Jake walked over to the horse and took the reins from her. "Let's get you settled into the house, Rose. We can talk about this later, after you've had something to eat and a chance to freshen up." Starving and exhausted, she welcomed that idea and let her Uncle Jake lead the rented animal down the short road to the ranch.

Aunt Caroline and Cousin Marie, who was named for Rose's mother, began to gush over Rose the minute they saw her. Rose told them why she'd left home, but they didn't press her for details. Every summer Rose and her cousin would be inseparable for several weeks, while Aunt Caroline became a healthy dose of the mother Rose never had. She would pamper and instruct, and set an example of how to be a proper lady. They were her only living relatives. Uncle Jake and Aunt Caroline were the best, and Marie was like a younger sister to her. That's why she'd come to them now, determined to build a life here in Reno. She'd decided on the train never to return to California and only wished that Wil would follow, but she dared not voice her hope, not even to cousin Marie.

Later that night after dinner Rose collapsed on the feather bed in the guestroom, exhausted. She studied the letter in the jeweled box, disappointed Uncle Jake had slipped out after dinner to check on the livestock. Someone knocked softly on the door and Rose let Marie in.

"What a beautiful box, Rose." Marie sat on the edge of the bed and picked it up, opening the hinged lid to reveal the treasured pieces of jewelry.

"Read this." Rose handed Marie the letter.

Her cousin stared at the delicate paper. "What is it?"

"It's a letter, never delivered."

Marie read while Rose admired a photo of her mother in a silver frame, glad she'd had the presence of mind to toss it into her suitcase before shutting it. Ann Marie looked happy and carefree in the picture. Her long strawberry hair hung loosely about her shoulders and there was a gleam in her eye, indicating an untamed spirit beneath the serious pose.

Marie looked up with moist eyes. "What an incredible story, Rose."

"I know. It's very tragic, isn't it?"

"Completely." Marie fell back onto the bed and stared at the ceiling. "What do you think happened? I mean, the night she died?"

"I don't know. I'm hoping Uncle Jake does."

"Father? He's never mentioned it. I know he had a terrible falling out with your father a long time ago." Marie's eyes darkened. "Rose, you aren't really my cousin. My father's brother Blaine isn't really your father. How sad!"

"I know, Marie. I thought of that. But we are more like sisters than cousins anyway. We are family no matter what!"

"Yes, yes we are!" Marie chimed in enthusiastically. "Besides, your real father was my father's best friend."

"Uncle Jake and William Mackenzie were best friends?" Rose sat up and looked at Marie. "The baby in the letter that William Mackenzie adopted is my boyfriend. His name is Wil. That's what Father and I fought about." Rose stood up and looked out the window, but all she could see were imaginings of that awful night long ago when her mother had died. "Why did Uncle Jake and William Mackenzie quit being best friends? What happened, Marie? Did it have to do with my mother's death?"

"Mother told me once," Marie added, "that the Bird of Paradise Casino we own used to be run by the Mackenzies. Why would they sell it to my father after everything that happened?"

Rose focused on her cousin's pretty face. "The Mackenzies owned the Bird of Paradise before Uncle Jake?"

Marie thought for a second, staring back at her cousin. "Yes. I'm sure of it. Mother and Father have often mentioned how indebted they are to the Mackenzie family. It was shortly after your mother's death that Father moved out here to run it and never went home again. And he doesn't speak to Uncle Blaine, who is his very own brother . . . or to your real father who had been his best friend all through school. I wonder why your grandfather, Bill Mackenzie, sold him the casino."

Rose sat back down on the bed. "Why yes, Bill Mackenzie was my grandfather, wasn't he? I wish I would have known that when he was alive. I'm just glad Father, or I suppose he is really *not* my father, has let me visit you every summer," Rose pointed out.

"That's true." Marie shrugged. "Maybe it's guilt. We are family you know, and Uncle Blaine never remarried."

Marie and Rose stared at each other. The same question was on both their minds. What happened in that barn over sixteen years ago?

The next day Rose walked boldly into the Bird of Paradise Casino and laid the letter on the table in front of Uncle Jake. He eyed it carefully and lifted his gaze to Rose. "What are you doing in here, honey? This is no place for a lady. And what's this for?"

The two other men drinking with Jake at the table got up quietly and left, after tipping their hats to Rose.

"It's a letter my mother wrote to your best friend, William Mackenzie." Rose sat down at the table.

Jake squirmed in his seat and glanced around the casino. "Are your Aunt Caroline and Marie still coming for the show tonight?"

"Yes. They'll be by later, to slip in the back room and watch Jenny Angelo sing, just like you told them they could. I've come early, Uncle Jake, to speak with you about my mother's death. I need to know what happened."

He unfolded the letter and held it close enough to read in the dim light. When he was finished he set it down as if a delicate treasure and slid it across the table toward Rose.

She stared at it lying before her and then flashed her troubled green eyes at the only man who could solve this mystery of her mother's past.

Jake sighed. "Rose, it's true that William Mackenzie was in love with your mother. And she loved him. But I never knew you were his kid."

"What happened that night, Uncle Jake?" Rose glanced about to be sure their conversation was private. "Did William Mackenzie find out that he was my father? Is that why he killed her? Out of anger?"

"No, Rose." Jake cleared his throat and looked around the half-filled room of gamblers, drinkers, and opportunists. "William wasn't angry with your mother that night. I can promise you that."

"Well what then?" Rose asked, her voice rising from frustration. "Did my father find out, and kill her thinking that he had been betrayed?"

"Rose . . ." Jake took her long slender hands into his large rough ones. "Your father doesn't know you're not his daughter. I'm sure of it, Rose. That secret died with your mother all those years ago."

"Why then, Uncle Jake?" Rose choked on her own emotion, and brought her voice down to a whisper. "Why did she die?"

"Rose, you know it was an accident." He couldn't look at her, staring at the pool players in the corner of the room instead. Jake fought hard to maintain his composure as he continued in an even tone. "The knife wasn't meant for her. It missed its mark. That's all."

With that said, Jake stood up. "I have to go, Rose. I got a business to run." He looked down at her, his eyes soft and sorry. "Forget about the past. There's nothing you can do to change it. Let it go, honey." He reached out and squeezed her hand gently. "You've just gotta move on, you hear me?"

Rose watched him cross the room, and thought about what a good man he was, strong and proud. He must have been a great friend to William Mackenzie. It hurt to think they hadn't seen each other all these years Uncle Jake was in Reno. William chose to stay in El Dorado. Maybe that's why the Mackenzie family sold the casino in Reno to Jake, because they'd gotten out of the saloon and gambling business, probably about the same time her mother had died. Mackenzies were now respected ranchers in El Dorado. It was hard to believe her real father had lived just a few ranches over her whole life.

Many lives had changed that night of her mother's death. She, for one, became motherless. William Mackenzie didn't know he was her father, and her supposed father, Blaine Bradey, was estranged from his brother, her Uncle Jake. The brothers hadn't spoken since the tragic accident. At least she had been allowed to visit Uncle Jake, Aunt Caroline, and Marie.

Right then Rose looked up to see her aunt and Marie arrive. They waved from the office door of the gambling casino, the only place a respectable woman would consider being in a casino. Fortunately it had a bird's eye view of the stage where Jenny Angelo would perform. Rose realized she should join them, just as she said she would, after begging Aunt Caroline to let her come early and speak with Uncle Jake. But as she stood from the table, she nearly fainted at the sight of Wil coming through the front door.

The tall, muscular young man glanced around the room, his eyes resting on Rose. He walked straight to her, as if on a mission. Wil touched her arm and kissed her cheek. "Rose, I can't believe you just ran off like that without letting me know."

They both sat down as he added, "You didn't even leave a note."

"I'm sorry Wil." Rose placed her hand on top of his. "Please forgive me. I . . . I didn't know what to say. I had a lot of thinking to do. How did you know where to find me?"

"I guessed. You always come visit your Uncle Jake in the summer, and I know how much you like him. I figured you ran away from your dad that night, when we were down by the creek and he came after us."

Rose reached into her handbag and pulled out the letter. "Read this."

"What is it?" Wil asked.

"It's a letter . . . that my mother wrote. To your father." Their eyes met.

"To *my* father?"

"Yes. Read it, Wil."

Rose watched his eyes as he read. Several times he looked up at her and fidgeted in his chair. When he was finished, he carefully refolded the thin, fragile stationery.

"They never told me." Wil pushed his hair back with a nervous hand. "I never knew they weren't my real parents."

"At least we don't share the same father." Rose squeezed his hand.

"True enough. Damn, Rose. The father I thought was mine is really yours."

"I know." They stared at each other, neither of them able to express all they felt about the letter, or each other.

Wil leaned closer to Rose, brushing the strawberry curls off her bare shoulders.

"I love you, Rose. I want to marry you. Here, in Reno."

"You would stay in Reno for me? Because I don't ever want to go back, Wil. I don't belong in El Dorado. My heart is here, and my future."

"I don't want to go back either. We can make a new beginning together."

They kissed lightly on the lips just as all six foot two inches of Wil's adopted father, and Rose's real father, William Mackenzie, entered the casino and strolled up to the bar. Wil looked dismayed that he'd obviously followed him all the way from El Dorado. How had he managed to keep his presence hidden on the train?

The teenagers watched as Uncle Jake and William stood frozen in time, staring one another down until finally they embraced. Aunt Caroline and Marie came dashing out of the office to greet them both, as if a spell had been broken. The men downed several shots, William glancing in Wil and Rose's direction only once. He tipped his hat at them, as if to say he meant no harm and didn't intend to interfere. Uncle Jake never looked their way at all.

No sooner had they all relaxed into merriment at this long overdue reunion when Blaine Bradey came crashing through the door. He swaggered to the middle of the room. A hushed tone spread throughout the casino as patrons observed the obviously drunk and agitated Blaine, looking purposefully about the room. He, too, Rose decided, must have been on the train arriving only hours ago. It was odd to stare at this man she had thought was her father, and now to know otherwise, to know that the man at the bar with Uncle Jake was her *real* father. A secret kept from him all these years, because of her mother's death preventing the delivery of the letter.

"Where are you, Jake? You bastard! I have come to collect my daughter."

Absolute quiet followed, with all eyes on Jake, standing at the bar with his back to Blaine.

"She doesn't want to go with you, Blaine. Why don't you come over here for a drink and we can talk about it?" Jake didn't turn to look at him. William Mackenzie didn't either, as he tugged on the brim of his hat and downed his shot, sliding the glass toward the bartender for a refill.

Aunt Caroline and Marie glanced nervously from Blaine, to Jake, and then to William. Customers began exiting the swank establishment until only a hardcore group of men remained, looking for either a resolution or revelation concerning Jake's mysterious past.

Blaine stared through blurry eyes at the frightened dark-haired beauties standing beside Jake. He had never laid eyes on his brother's wife and child before. Then he scanned the room and rested his vision on Wil and Rose huddled together at the corner table, looking like star-crossed lovers.

"You're a traitorous son-of-a-bitch, Jake! It's one thing for you to befriend Mackenzie trash. But I'll be damned if I let my daughter do the same!"

"That's enough, Blaine." William Mackenzie turned slowly around to face his long time adversary. "Jake here didn't get Wil and Rose together. They did that on their own."

"Shut-up Mackenzie. You no good murdering bastard," Blaine hissed, hate flashing from his narrowly slit eyes.

Jake turned to face Blaine. He began walking toward his brother when Blaine pulled a gun on him, causing Jake to freeze midway across the room. Aunt Caroline and Marie gasped as William Mackenzie tucked them behind the counter, where they crouched to watch with worried eyes. Wil and Rose huddled together at their corner table as the few other men in the room downed their drinks and shifted their weight, eager for what promised to be a great show.

"Put the gun away, Blaine. Let's you and I step outside and deal with this man to man, or brother to brother as the case would be," Jake reasoned, standing calmly in the middle of the room.

"My fight isn't with you, brother. It's with that lowlife friend of yours." Blaine looked sharply toward the bar, while keeping the gun pointed at Jake. "Get your ass over here, William Mackenzie! It's about time you paid for murdering my wife!"

"Put away your gun, Blaine. And then I'd be happy to have it out with you in the street. Just you and me," William Mackenzie replied smoothly, standing straight and confident at the bar.

Blaine shouted with slurred speech, "Why'd you kill her, Mackenzie? Just because she was rightfully mine, and you didn't have any claim on her? What kind of bitter scum takes revenge on a woman just because she never loved him?" Blaine swayed slightly as he belted out his hate-filled words and waved the gun around. "Is that why you killed her . . . because she chose me? What kind of reason is that to leave Rose here with no mama?" He nodded his head toward the corner table, where Rose slowly stood and pulled the letter from her handbag.

"You know why we fought, Blaine. If you hadn't been trying to *rape your own wife*, I wouldn't have needed to beat the crap out of you!" William hissed.

"I had every right to show my woman that it was time to be a proper wife to me." Blaine stared at William, his gun aimed at Jake. "Our child had been born and Anne Marie was good as new again. Time to do her wifely duties." Blaine grinned and then grimaced. "Our child is proof that Ann Marie loved me! Me and only me! You just thought she loved you. It was wishful thinking, you sorry bastard."

"Stop it, Father!" Rose demanded, standing rigid at the table. She was a vision of youthful beauty in her green velvet dress, the strawberry curls bouncing on her pale shoulders as she unfolded the letter and held it out toward Blaine, his gun still aimed at Jake.

"Mother *did* love William Mackenzie. She never *stopped* loving him," Rose said adamantly, waving the letter in the air and glancing at William. "*He's* my father. I'm a *Mackenzie*." Her voice broke slightly, but she continued. "And Wil here, *isn't*. He was adopted." She glanced at Wil. "And he wants to marry me, despite the fact that I am as you say . . . *Mackenzie trash.*"

A rush of excited mumbling roared through the room. Aunt Caroline looked at Marie, whose eyes betrayed knowledge of the secret she had read in the hidden letter.

"That's a lie. All lies!" Blaine yelled gruffly, waving the gun through the air.

"No, father. It's the truth. And it's all here in this letter, written by Mother herself."

"William Mackenzie killed your mother, child!" Blaine waved the gun at William. "Are you going to forgive him for that?"

"No, Blaine," Jake interrupted. "William didn't kill Ann Marie." He glanced at Rose and Wil. "It's time the truth was known, once and for all."

"*Jake* . . ." William said in protest.

"No. It's time to tell the truth. Rose has a right to know." He glanced at his niece and then looked Blaine straight in the eye. "*I killed Ann Marie that night . . . not William.*"

No one moved or even blinked, except for Rose, who brought her hands up to her face and shook her head in disbelief.

"*You?* You killed my wife? *My own brother?*" Blaine mumbled.

"Yes, Blaine. I saw you and Rose quarreling at the charity ball that night, and I saw her speak briefly with William. Then she slipped out the back and you followed. When William left too, I thought there might be trouble."

Jake paused and tugged at his hat, staring blankly into empty space and sighing deeply, the story pulling from him pain and remorse kept buried all this time.

"When I reached the barn, you and William were struggling. Ann Marie watched, shocked and dazed. But then you pulled a gun, and would have killed William Mackenzie in cold blood." Jake looked into his brother's face again. "I could tell by the hate in your eyes. So I threw my knife. It was only meant to hit your trigger arm, but then William knocked you out and the knife sailed on past. *Right into Ann Marie.*" He looked squarely at his drunken brother. "If Ann Marie hadn't sprung forward when you drew the gun on William, she'd still be alive."

Blaine appeared to be quite shaken up, and with a tortured look on his face he cocked the hammer on his gun. Everyone flinched at the eerie sound in the silent casino.

"Go ahead, Blaine. Shoot me. I deserve it. Killing an innocent woman. It's inexcusable, what I did. My brother's wife . . . and my best friend's true love." Jake looked at William. "I even left the scene of the crime and let my best friend clean up after me."

"It was my idea for you to go, Jake," William interjected. "There wasn't any reason to involve you. It was my fight. Mine and Blaine's." He paused and looked at Rose. "Nothing was going to bring Ann Marie back. *It was just a tragic accident.*"

William looked sharply at Blaine. "One that never would have happened if you hadn't tried to *rape* your own wife."

Blaine turned slightly and angled the gun at William. "You always won everything, didn't you, Mackenzie?" He shook his head slowly. "In school you were the fastest and the smartest. My own brother liked you more than he liked me." Blaine glanced at Jake.

"And then the girl I had a crush on fell head over heels for *you*." He began to chuckle. "Well, you can have them all, Mackenzie . . . you bastard. My murdering brother, your illegitimate daughter . . . this sin haven of a casino your father set my brother up in for saving your worthless neck."

He uttered a sinister chuckle, raising the gun to his head, touching the tip to his temple. "But you'll never have your lover back, my whore of a wife who slept with you before our wedding night, and then let me believe that Rose was mine." He looked up, laughing long and hard, the gun still at his temple. Then with a somber expression he glared at William. "I'll tell Ann Marie hi for you, when I meet up with her in hell."

Blaine pulled the trigger.

Aunt Caroline and Marie screamed and hugged each other, hiding their faces from the hideous sight. Rose wept silently into Wil's chest, his arms tight around her. Jake and William scrambled to take his pulse, their heads bowed in silence and shock. Onlookers shook their heads and mumbled among themselves.

It was barely four weeks later when Uncle Jake made a toast to William, and the memory of Ann Marie, at Wil and Rose's wedding on his ranch. Rose kept the jeweled box that belonged to her mother and grandmother, for her own daughter Ann, who was born a year later.

Every now and then Rose would open the jeweled box and read what her mother had written on the fragile stationery. Rose hoped her mother knew those heartfelt words of truth had finally been heard, and she looked forward to telling Ann about all the lives forever changed because of that one, hidden letter.

longing

i long for everything
about you
the softness of your skin
kindness in your eyes . . .
your gentle words
but most of all
the warmth of your love
heat of your passion . . .
a consuming desire
the miracle
of your presence

love is wanting to see
your smile . . .
hear your voice
talk with you face to face
love is
needing you now
wanting you always
thinking of you . . .
every moment
of every day

skyward

From the beach Gwyneth watched a large purple sail float across the sky, straining her eyes so as not to lose sight of the person dangling beneath it. She wondered what the odds of crashing were. Gwyneth hadn't done anything that would qualify as daring since her husband Charles died of cancer several years ago, after a fast and fatal affair with the ugly disease. Before that they sailed the San Juans every June in their twenty-four-foot rig and were no strangers to wilderness backpacking, often hiking up steep rugged slopes in the Colorado or Canadian Rockies.

Why not do it? Gwyneth reasoned, hoping to talk herself into the ludicrous idea. This was Aruba. When would she take a cruise in the Caribbean again? Gwyneth watched people parasail above the dazzling turquoise sea and float skyward effortlessly for one long breathless thrill. She wanted her own taste of that thrill.

"Let's do it!" Gwyneth decided, looking over at Brianna.

"Do what?" her college-bound daughter asked, sizzling under the hot sun in a pink bikini.

"Go parasailing."

"Seriously?" Brianna sat up and looked at her mother.

"Why not? It isn't like we'll get another opportunity anytime soon."

"You'll freak. You might actually get wet, Mom, or have to use those subtle muscles you work so hard at developing in the gym."

"Very funny. I don't mind getting wet, in fact, I've already been in for a dip. You haven't left the towel you're lying on."

"Okay, well, if you chicken out or scream I'll never let you live it down, and no blaming me if you hate it. This was your idea."

"Agreed. You either." Gwyneth grinned.

"Hey, let's remember I'm a real jock. You're the pretend one." Brianna grabbed an ice-cold water from the cooler. "When do you want to do this?"

Gwyneth stared into the sky where several of the silky orange and yellow sails were bobbing in the slight tropical breeze. She took a deep breath and inhaled the faint scent of Plumeria flowers growing just beyond the beach.

"Now."

"Okay, let's go then." Brianna stood up and began brushing sand off her skin, while Gwyneth tied a long flowered scarf around her waist. Together they walked the short distance to the makeshift booth where the parasailing boat docked. All morning Gwyneth had watched the boat hoist people up and then bring them in for a perfect landing. *Every time. Piece of cake. Nothing to it really, no danger involved, just gutsy nerve and a hundred dollars burning a hole in your pocket, begging you to do something memorable for once . . .*

They signed up for the next run in half an hour. Neither would admit their stomachs were queasy at the thought of floating above the sea and through the sky.

As Gwyneth waded in the shallow water near the shore she realized everything she did was out of habit and routine. It was as if her spirit died with Charles. He always had impulsive ideas like taking dinner down to the boat on a balmy August night, or running along the beach in a warm summer downpour. She missed him.

At least the searing pain of her grief had faded to a dull ache. For the past year she'd been seeing Matthew. He wasn't one to run in a summer shower, for fear of catching a cold. Maybe that's why she hadn't agreed to marry him yet. He was just a little too cautious. And then there was her work. It was unbelievable how many hours she'd put in since the funeral. Who wants spare time to dwell on what's missing from their life?

"Mom, look!" Brianna pointed at the flawless landing of someone parasailing. They watched the boat head for shore, their eagerness laced with a hint of fear. Soon they were ushered on deck and put at ease by the smiling parasail experts, with bronzed chests and knee length swim-wear covered in bright green foliage and fuchsia blossoms.

Gwyneth tried to focus while they walked through the setup, take off, and landing with Brianna harnessed in first. Gwyneth asked her daredevil daughter if she was sure she wanted to go through with it, but the huge grin on Brianna's face was the only answer she needed.

"Pay attention Mom, 'cause you're next!"

"Right. I'll watch your every move." Gwyneth smiled despite her sudden hesitation about the whole idea. Her heart pounded like the island drums had done when welcoming their cruise ship. She soon felt more exhilaration than fear watching her daughter maneuver effortlessly through the cloudless blue sky, ending her adventure in the air with a perfect landing.

Gwyneth found herself harnessed in before she could change her mind. Strangely, her earlier fears were replaced with peaceful anticipa-tion as she rose up into the air, the wind whipping by her like a playful kitten. The view along the shoreline was more spectacular than she had imagined it would be. She suddenly felt akin to every creature in winged flight. Oh to never be grounded again! If she could just fly away into the pre-dusk sky and not look back.

Gwyneth braced herself for the landing and felt confident it would equal the dreamlike state of her flawless flight, until a careless wake-boarder clipped off the parasailing cruise boat and drastically cut her landing short. Everything felt surreal to Gwyneth as her eyes stared into the water fast approaching. Too fast. She was going to take a plunge into the sea, feet first. And she did, with the silky sail strewn atop her when she surfaced, like a spider web encasing its prey. Gasping for air she gulped mostly saltwater instead, before sinking again despite her bulky life vest.

A sea turtle approached her from below looking somewhat dazed. The gentle giant stared her in the eye, and somehow Gwyneth believed everything would be okay. Weren't sea turtles good luck? She kicked upward with all her might, afraid her lungs might burst otherwise. As she surfaced this time the sail was not there and hands were reaching out to her as Brianna shouted, "Mom! Are you okay?"

Choking, spitting, and inhaling air all at once, it was several minutes before Gwyneth could answer, and by then it was apparent she would live to tell her tale. Everyone helped her back into the boat while doling out towels, tissues, and apologies all at the same time.

Brianna was the most apologetic of all. "I'm so sorry, Mom. Can you ever forgive me?" she asked, when finally they were left alone with spicy rum-laced drinks for the trip to shore.

"Sorry for what, honey? Not everything in life can be predictable. The point is we're both okay, more than okay. It was fabulous. I haven't felt this alive in a long time." Gwyneth patted Brianna on the knee. "I've missed taking risks. I forgot what it feels like to do something thrilling."

Brianna's eyes widened. "That's it? You're not upset or anything?"

"Not at all. Did I tell you I collided with the most amazing sea turtle down there, under the water? I actually thought I'd drown until making his acquaintance."

They both laughed, enjoying the dazzling sunset cruise extended just for them, compliments of the crew. Everyone onboard wanted a happy finale to their parasailing excursion. Gwyneth was suddenly struck with the same determination to have a wonderful finale to her own life. She did, after all, still have decades of quality living to consider.

Picturing the sea turtle eye to eye brought her face to face with desire for excitement again. Before they stepped foot on the soft white sand Gwyneth had made plans to break it off with Matthew, and leave her job. On the way back to the cruise ship she bought a small jade sea turtle from a trinket shop near the docks. It would be a memento of her para-sailing adventure in paradise, and a cornerstone to the future.

Gwyneth was ready to aim for something skyward, and she might even parasail again . . . since she didn't quite have that landing down yet.

the rainforest

a reckoning presented by a serpent

Amelia stared at Emily with a look of dismay as the tour guide described poisonous plants and creatures to avoid. Why did she let Emily pick the day trips off the cruise ship? Her best friend since third grade had developed quite an appetite for adventure. Standing in a hot humid jungle waiting to hike a trail filled with all sorts of possible disasters was not Amelia's idea of a relaxing vacation.

At least it would take her mind off of Kate, dying a slow painful death back home in Colorado. Amelia hoped this cruise would help clear her head, so she could make a sound decision about the fate of her little sister's kids, Max and Maddie.

"Please, people, use common sense, and *do not* wander away from the trails, or leave your partner's side at any time." The tour guide looked straight at Amelia, whose discomfort must have shown. She felt out of place with these botanist types, who found giant hairy spiders and lethal frogs a turn-on. Perhaps she should have forfeited the cruise, even though it was paid for months in advance, and Emily had insisted she needed the time away to think.

"Remember not to touch anything without asking me first. Brush along the trail is harmless, but even a few inches over could be a poisonous plant or bug."

Amelia hoped she would not be adding physical discomfort to match her mental agony. She was glad she'd taken the advice in the brochure on ship and worn her lightweight Nike pants instead of shorts, to spare skin contact with sticky, stinging things in foliage or flying form.

"Come on, Amelia, pay attention," Emily whispered, pulling her by the arm as they brought up the rear of their hiking group.

"Okay, sorry," she mumbled, happy to follow Emily and not have to be on the lookout for brightly colored frogs that carry little sacks of poison or spiders with deadly bites. If only Emily could clear the cluttered trail back home for her, too. Amelia cared deeply about what might happen to her sister's kids. She just didn't feel adequate to parent them herself. What did she know about kids? It was exactly why she didn't have any.

Delicate blossoms on lush plants lined the trail. It was such an exquisite wonderland! Amelia parted a few broad, waxy leaves and wiggled closer, spying a perfect white flower. It was forming honey-colored beads of moisture. Mesmerized by the beautiful bloom, Amelia hung back from the group and inhaled the sweet perfume of it, reaching out to touch the supple petals. When she glanced up, Emily was disappearing around the bend with the tall, broad shouldered man who was the only real botanist on the hike. It appeared to Amelia that her best friend was more than a little smitten with him. So much for sticking with your trail partner!

Amelia missed her husband. She wanted to share this unique plant with Connor, who was sitting beside her dying sister back home in the hospital. How could her little sister be dying? At only thirty-two she should be invincible. Kate had always been so healthy and full of energy. She grew up romping through the fields behind their sprawling family home, while Amelia had sat in the tree fort and read all day.

What would happen to Kate's two little kids, not even half raised? Picturing the blond and freckled eight-year-old Max and his little sister Maddie with the bottomless brown eyes, made her own swell with tears. There was Austin of course, but he was pointless as a father. He divorced Kate shortly after the cancer got unpleasant, and then high-tailed it off to New York with no forwarding address. Run chicken run, Amelia thought. Just as well . . . out of sight, out of mind.

A brightly colored cockatoo cawed loudly on a nearby branch and Amelia jumped, relieved to see it was a feathered friend without poisonous secretions of any type. Cocking its head to the right, the exotic bird studied Amelia with a round emerald eye. It would have been hard to say which was more curious about the other. Amelia suddenly realized with dread that Emily had rounded the bend with the botanist too long ago to catch up. Drat, she thought. Just my luck to be left behind in a rainforest!

"Now what," she said out loud, while staring at the path ahead, wondering if she dare follow it in hopes of catching up to the group. Thickly intertwined greenery all but camouflaged it. Did she want to trudge through that undergrowth alone, with no one ahead to scout for spiders or frogs, and any number of other creepy, crawly, and scaly things? She shivered involuntarily at the thought.

They'll come back for me, Amelia reasoned. Any minute now Emily would miss her. The smart thing to do would be to stay put and wait. She was hot and sweaty, and the dense humidity was making her breathing heavy. Amelia had been standing still long enough to attract every flying creature within a half-mile radius. They began to swarm near her head as she batted them away.

Amelia decided pacing along the narrow path would make her less easy prey for hungry insects. She walked back and forth in front of the gnarly branch that held the cockatoo. The brilliantly colored bird still viewed her suspiciously with one round emerald eye at a time. She finished her bottled water and out of frustration crushed the flimsy plastic. The trees were instantly alive with hoots and caws and chirping, a true chorus of jungle music.

Was it the offending screech of crushed plastic that set them off? Or was it feeding time in the forest? Amelia had no idea why the feathered group was being so vocal. She wondered how long it would take Emily to hike back here and pick her up, because her nerves were becoming a bit frazzled. Sitting on a nearby stump, weariness settled into her bones. The day had been completely out of her comfort zone thus far and it was taking a toll on her.

It seemed to Amelia that everything in her life was out of her comfort zone of late. Nothing was a pleasant walk in the woods. Everything was a jungle to inch through with fear and trepidation. She had wanted to quit her job back home and begin her own computer graphics business, but her boss had threatened lawsuits if she took clients with her. And there was the risk of eating up savings while trying to make it on her own. Now her sister was dying and had nobody to raise Max and Maddie.

It felt wrong to worry about possibly stealing clients and squandering life savings when your little sister's life was being swept out from under her. And how could she not openly embrace raising those two adorable little kids, tied to her by blood? She had bonded with each of them the moment they were born. A more attentive aunt did not exist. But parenting was a different beast. Had she thought she'd be successful at it, she would have considered a family of her own.

Connor's words echoed in her head even louder than the buzzing creatures, which had found her again now that she was immobile. *We could turn the bonus room above the garage into two bedrooms and a bath. And if you ran your computer graphics business from home you'd be there for the kids after school.*

Amelia angrily repositioned her ponytail, smoothing back the hairs falling into her face from stalking through the rainforest and batting bugs in the air. She wiped her sweaty brow with the back of her hand and glanced repeatedly at the trail, hoping to catch a glimpse of her rescue mission, surely only seconds away.

"I wish it were that simple, Connor," she said out loud, scowling at the thick leaves protruding all around her in every shape and size. The muggy air oozed sweet fragrances. Creatures hidden within lush plants lavishly growing about cawed and chirped an answer to her question. The harmonious chatter of these forest foragers was soothing, in a disconcerting way, perhaps similar to a soldier in the trenches being comforted by battle sounds in the far distance. She left her stump chair to lean against the tree with the cockatoo and was soon lost in thought.

It was a short-lived introspective moment.

Amelia cringed as she felt something slither onto her neck. It was a snake crawling off a tree branch. She wanted to grab the slimy scaly creature and fling it across the path but something deep inside caused her to freeze. Intuitively she felt it might attack her with a deadly bite unless she grabbed it exactly right and that would take some thought, never having had a snake crawl onto her before. Within seconds it coiled around her thin fragile neck, making it hard to breathe. The cockatoo squawked loudly and flew away.

Amelia decided that bite or no bite, she needed to pull it off her neck. Wrapping her fingers around the snake, she yanked at it with all her might to no avail. Instinctively she thrust her body back against the tree trunk, still pulling with all her might, hoping if she banged the slimy serpent hard enough, it would remove its grip.

Realizing that wasn't working, she gasped for air and slid down along the rough bark, hoping it would release itself. The snake fell to the ground with a thud, its shiny green body wiggling quickly away through tall grass at her feet.

Amelia gasped to fill her lungs with heavy jungle air and considered the irony of it all. Worried about spiders and frogs, she hadn't considered an attack by a snake. Sweating profusely she stared at the tree where it all happened. Had she been bitten? It didn't feel like it. Although shaky and bruised, she seemed to be fine. Who would have raised Max and Maddie if she'd died? That question answered everything.

In the next instant she heard a familiar voice and looked up to see a worried Emily skipping over branches and dodging green foliage. "Amelia! Where were you? We were all so worried!" They embraced in a hug of relief.

Emily looked sheepish. "I was so upset when we noticed you weren't behind us anymore." She glanced at the botanist, waiting on the trail ahead.

"Well, I'm fine. And I've made up my mind about Max and Maddie."
"What about them?"
"If I can survive the rainforest all alone, I can raise those kids and

start my own design business, too. Why not? It will be an adventure worth taking, never a dull moment at least."

"That's wonderful, Amelia. I think you're doing the right thing, giving those kids a home. Who would have thought a little old rainforest could help you decide that." Emily grinned.

"I guess it's taught me that risks are worth taking if you want to experience life to the fullest, and besides, I think I'm more capable than I realized."

"I see," Emily said, with a puzzled look on her face.

Amelia smiled. This little bend in the trail was exactly what she'd needed. It gave her the courage to face life head on. She would always be grateful to Emily for that, and to the botanist who'd pulled Emily away. It had allowed Amelia to consider Kate's daily struggle with obstacles greater than those witnessed in this jungle. Surely she could put her little sister's mind at rest about who would raise her children once the green snake of fate had squeezed out Kate's last breath.

While she hiked back through the rainforest Amelia brainstormed how to begin her new design business. She couldn't wait to e-mail Connor from the cruise ship and tell him about the delicate white flower she'd seen, and to give him a thumbs-up for clearing out the bonus room. After all, it would be important to have it ready when Max and Maddie moved in.

roatan: a travel journal

penning thoughts about a perplexing paradise

When landing in San Pedro Sula, Honduras, I am reminded by my surroundings that I am in a third world country. The local airlines compete for commuter customers to the island of Roatan no differently than taxi drivers in LA. I soon board a twin-engine plane small and worn enough to make me nervous, but the ride is enchanting as we fly over an emerald sea framed in white sand.

Welcome to your island adventure I whisper under my breath as it lands.

My newlywed daughter, Ava, is waiting at baggage claim. Her face lights up when she sees me and soon we are locked in a tight hug. I feel at home with her despite being three thousand miles and half a continent from California. We grab the luggage and walk to the parking lot, both giggling like young girls.

It flashes through my mind how I will never forgive Max for taking my daughter so far away. His father, Jack Conner, has bought oceanfront real estate on the island and Max designs vacation homes to build on their property. Ava is the sales manager. Jack hovers backstage holding the purse strings to fund permits and orchestrate other essential power plays. The right politics are key for allowing their home building business to flourish and grow in a third world country with no true concept of free enterprise.

Max has a gift for designing edgy architecture that somehow blends with native ambiance. They sell these exquisite vacation homes to rich Europeans and Americans, showing how the ways of the world have not changed that much since Columbus sailed for India. I worry that bitterness over a rich American purchasing land and speckling the beachfront with privileged homes will compromise Max and Ava's safety in this third world nation. There is no doubt Jack Conner's wellbeing is at risk. Even I know that without anyone mentioning it.

"Max had to make an unavoidable trip last minute," Ava explains as we walk to the truck. I can barely catch my breath in the hot humid air and stop to observe how short stubby palm trees surround the little shack of an airport. "July and August are the worst," she adds. "Any other month is better, but this is our least busy time for building or selling, so I can take off work and visit with you."

"It's okay." I smile at her, happy to be here.

Ava piles my baggage into the back of the pickup. "Max is selling the SUV," she explains. "Gas prices have become exorbitant, making our Land Rover a bad investment. He found someone through the Internet to buy it. They live in Texas."

Ava starts the engine in the truck and continues to tell me how entrepreneurs such as themselves are victim to astronomical island prices for anything imported, which is practically everything other than coconuts and white sand.

We exit the airport onto a narrow road and dodge locals who walk slowly down the gravel street side by side, as if fearless. Ava swerves to miss the native-born pedestrians and honks at oncoming traffic. Vehicles move at a fast pace despite the death defying curves we encounter. We mostly pass dated jeeps and trucks that have been ridden at least as hard as the commuter plane I just exited and the pickup now holding us hostage. Regular low-clearance cars are mainly well-worn taxis, which Ava points out are quite impractical considering the size and frequency of ruts in the road, and how fast a torrential downpour can flood the streets.

We arrive at the house, which is a square-framed home built on stilts overlooking the ocean. It is surrounded by a generous wraparound porch nestled beside lush greenery and boasts several inviting hammocks. While peering over the rail, Ava tells me their landlord, Miss

Alene, lives in the only other house we can see from the property.

One can almost lean over the railing and pluck bananas growing in little green bunches on Miss Alene's trees. I want to pluck them, as I have never picked a banana straight from the tree before. "You can't eat them right away," Ava says. "You hang them on hooks until they ripen."

Hummingbirds flutter by me and cock their heads at my computer, which I have setup at a rattan table. Some of the hovering birds are a deep purple, while others have bright orange bellies. A green lizard about five inches long crawls across the deck railing. His throat expands and contracts like a red balloon as he breathes in and out.

I stare at the ocean view from the porch and observe that it has no waves. It is just a mass of gently moving blue out there. Soon I am completely enthralled by cooing doves, hidden in flowering bushes scattered between house and beach. The brilliant blooms on the bushes have attracted a variety of butterflies, many as bright and bold as the flowers.

I try to block out brilliant blooms full of butterflies, lizards with red balloon throats, and an ocean so blue it makes my heart do flip-flops, focusing instead on an article I need to finish for a magazine in the States. Ava is whipping up guacamole in the kitchen, made from the buttery green fruit dripping off avocado trees all around the property.

I hear footsteps and look up from my keyboard to see a tall broad-shouldered man walking toward the porch from across the way. I wonder if this could be Mr. Nash, whom Ava says owns the Internet Café just down the road. He appears to be of Spanish descent, but is not a short Honduran. He is probably six-foot-two and although a lovely bronze color, not nearly as dark as the natives. I stand to greet him as he extends his arm across the porch rail to shake my hand.

"Welcome to our little island. I am Thomas Nash." Mr. Nash tips his white straw hat to me. I can't help but stare at his large brown eyes. They seem to be twinkling with much mischief, probably as much done as waiting to do.

"You must be Ava's mother." Mr. Nash smiles broadly. "You look just like her," he adds, his deep voice sizzling with charm.

"Yes, I am here for a visit." I smile and add, "I'm already in love with your seductive shores."

"Well, it is paradise," Mr. Nash admits. "But be careful. Danger lurks just beneath the breezy palms. Never know when a coconut might fall on your head. Gotta watch where you walk." He laughs low and long, showing perfect white teeth, then tips his white straw hat and saunters away, making long strides to the gravel road.

My eyes wander to the coconuts in trees at the far side of the deck. Ava has told me how islanders whack the top off with a machete and drain the water, which some drink for medicinal purposes. Women grate the meat and mash it in a bowl. They use the sweet heavy milk for soups and breads. I like this vision better than imagining coconuts mashing someone's head in.

"Was that Mr. Nash?" Ava asks, while setting down a tray with freshly fried tortilla strips and spicy guacamole.

"Yes. He's quite a charmer, isn't he?" I stare into the distance as I comment, waiting for him to reappear as abruptly as he had left.

"Thomas Nash is charming, yes, but he can be quite frightening, if you cross him."

"Why would anyone want to cross him?"

Ava shrugs. "I've just heard stories. He's never been anything but cordial to me personally."

"What kind of stories?" I look at my daughter while dipping a warm tortilla strip into creamy homemade guacamole.

"Well, they say if you owe him money he can be scarier than a pack of dogs chasing you."

We drop the subject and Ava begins to tell me all about the woes of building on the island. How hard it was to get permits and how lots of money was exchanged under tables for everything. There was even a land dispute over what Jack Conner had purchased. Apparently a few long-established native-born families believed they had rights to the land that was sold out from under them.

My concerns become real fears as she tells me about delivering pay for the workers at the end of each week. Always cash. But this past Friday Ava had been in Coexen Hole with a potential client when the week's pay needed to be dispersed among the building crew. A part-time secretary delivered the money, only to be shot at several times. She'd dropped the bag of cash and run. The armed thieves stole it of course, but fortunately the secretary, although scared out of her wits, was not harmed.

What if it had been Ava, and they'd hit their target?

I have a sleepless night full of masked robbers and red-throated lizards the size of coconuts, falling from trees and being shot as they scamper away.

My second morning, after eating thick island bacon and thin-yolked eggs from local chickens, Ava and I decide to visit Anthony's Key, one of the most famous resorts in the Caribbean. It's just a mile down the beach, a stone's throw from Ava's quaint little house on the stilt beams. We walk along the shore with our bare feet in the surf but part of the way we must leave the ocean and cut through a small island village. Women are hanging clothes on lines strung between narrow rows of houses while barefoot children play chase in the front yards. Scraggly dogs follow along and bark occasionally as we pass by on the gravel street.

When we reach the resort we are allowed to enter without any questions only because our skin is white, and we look wealthy. Anyone visiting the island from a developed country is considered rich. Natives, born and raised in Roatan, go to their graves without ever seeing the trained dolphins and groomed beaches. Somehow, this reality diminishes the natural beauty of our setting. It is a heavy invisible cloud that refuses to let songbirds soar.

The water at Anthony's Key shimmers a translucent green. Two dolphins swim over to say hello as we stand on the walkway and admire the view. One offers us seaweed between his teeth. We throw the seaweed a few times and the dolphin brings it back remarkably fast, darting like a bullet through the shallow water.

In the afternoon we take a taxi to West End, appropriately named because it is at the west end of the forty-mile-long island. The majority of boats are docked there. Across the rutted dirt road from the boat docks and sandy beach, we browse through little shops that sell local island jewelry, pottery, and hand-sewn quilts. For dinner we have rotisserie chicken at an open-air bar, while two tamed macaws kept by the owner entertain us from the porch railing. Chickens peck the ground nearby and I wonder how many minutes ago my dinner was doing the same.

Later that evening we walk onto the pier in front of Ava's rental home to watch the sunset. I ask Ava why the pier is so crooked and she tells me Hurricane Mitch had his way with it a few years ago.

"Do they have hurricanes here often?" I ask.

Ava smiles. "There are lots of warnings during hurricane season, but most are near misses—they end up being bad storms instead."

I shiver at the thought and think about Ava's little house on stilts, not far at all from the unprotected shore. No wonder her landlord's home is set back, protected by trees and brush.

The pier is maybe two hundred feet straight out, and the sea is so clear you can view a variety of tiny fish along the way. We end our evening watching spectacular colors bleed together in the sky, and I realize that Roatan is as complex and yet as stunningly simple as this sunset all ablaze.

After a night of air-conditioned slumber thanks to the ancient window machines used only for sleeping, I awaken to a chorus of doves cooing relentlessly. The smell of Honduran coffee, which is decidedly among the best in the world, is enticing me from the bed. I find Ava already busy in the kitchen frying more of the thick smoked bacon and thin-yolked eggs.

"Why are the yolks so thin?" I ask.

"It's their island diet."

"What do they eat on the island that's different?"

Ava laughs. "They're fed rotting fruit. We have a lot of fruit trees on the island and it often can't be utilized quickly enough."

We decide that rotten fruit gives their eggs amazing flavor to offset the thin yolks. After a second cup of the luxurious coffee we hurriedly dress and walk to the Internet Café, suddenly eager to check e-mail. Ava is hoping to hear from Max, and I need to catch up on work correspondence.

Thomas Nash is standing on his covered porch watching us walk up the dusty gravel road.

"Good morning to you!" he bellows with his seductive island accent, eyes twinkling beneath the white straw hat.

"Good morning to you too!" I yell, stopping to soak in the view of this tall angular man standing on his porch of rough-hewn logs that fit the ambiance of the jungle environment. There's a wooden table with four chairs behind him, and a couple picturesque hand-carved rockers on either side.

"What brings you down this way so early in the morning? Is it to get one of my tasty pecan rolls fresh from the oven, or to check your e-mail from the States?"

Thomas Nash chuckles.

"No hurry for e-mail," Ava answers. "I think a pecan roll would be perfect right about now." She leans into me and whispers under her breath, "I think Mr. Nash has taken a liking to you." I can feel my face flush as we are seated at the table on the porch. Thomas serves us strong Honduran coffee in thick cream-colored mugs and a roll covered in pecan-sprinkled frosting. It's giving off a sweet scent of confectioners' sugar mixed with butter and I want to devour it instantly, but opt for manners and small bites.

Ava and I savor this luscious treat and listen to Thomas Nash tell us a few island stories about lost treasure and missing mainlanders. His stories would have been amusing if not for my concern about Jack, Max, and Ava having their somewhat controversial entrepreneurial venture on this tiny postcard stretch of pearl white sand. Perhaps this is the real treasure Mr. Nash is referring to, and the missing islanders those who would have the audacity to claim it for their own, regardless of what they may have paid, and precisely because of whom they paid it to.

After checking e-mail we play cards on the porch with Thomas, who flashes those twinkling eyes from under his white straw hat throughout the games of rummy he consistently wins. I wonder if Mr. Nash wins at all his games, and how high the stakes may be in some.

Thomas owns this oceanfront property next door to Ava's landlord, Miss Alene. Even though their properties touch, it takes a half-mile gravel road to walk from one to the other.

For the evening my daughter and I take a taxi into West End and watch the sun set over the ocean at Sundowner Bar, a gathering for divers from foreign shores. Most of them have British accents and chain smoke cigarettes selling for a mere eighty cents a pack. A jet-black islander converses with them, claiming to be an African descendant from slaves the British brought over to work sugar plantations.

While enjoying our rum-and-Cokes at the open-air bar some native musicians serenade us with universal love songs and we pay them with Honduran money, called lempiras. Eighteen lempiras equal one American dollar.

"There's Jack!" Ava points to someone at the far end of the bar. He sees her at the same time. Jack Conner stands to pay for his drink and works his way through the crowd to where we are. They hug and she introduces me. After shaking my hand he orders a round of drinks and nods at a table just opening up a few feet away. We sit down and immediately seem as if old friends, the three of us—laughing, joking, and discussing the idiosyncrasies of Roatan.

I never ask why Jack did not return to the States for Max and Ava's wedding, or why he chose to cajole them three thousand miles away from home to begin their newlywed lives. I don't ask, because I know the answers. His ex-wife has a warrant out for his arrest, hoping to regain restitution for the assets he swindled her out of in their divorce proceeding: assets to fund his island endeavors. His ill-gotten gains grow even murkier as they become beachfront condos built by the sweat of native islanders, but affordable only for rich foreigners.

On the flip side of this, the islanders are paid well to build the homes, and the homes will bring money to the island because the Europeans and Americans who purchase them will spend their money while here. Of course, there are always two sides to any divorce, and some see Jack's absconding with liquefied marital assets as justified, if not quite legal.

Max and Ava are newly out of college and starry eyed for travel. More importantly, they don't plan to stay. Max wants to gain experience with designing homes and Ava with marketing. They see it as an opportunity to help Jack while growing in their careers and experiencing an adventure. They plan to return to the States in a couple years to buy their own property and begin a family.

I try to balance all this information swimming in my consciousness while our round of drinks turns into two and then three. Jack Conner is charming to say the least. Well built with sandy hair and tanned skin slightly burned beneath the eyes, from too much glare under his ball hat while fishing every chance he gets.

Sailing and deep sea diving stories fall delightfully from his tongue and it becomes obvious he has little interest in other aspects of Roatan, besides building vacation homes on her shores of pearl white sand.

"Saw an alligator on the north bank," Jack says low and slow, as if he wouldn't want others to hear. This shore secret is churned up after hours of drinking dark rum. He stares straight at Ava, as if he dares her to dispute it.

"I never heard of just one alligator being anywhere," Ava says.

"What's on the north shore?" I ask.

"Not much really," Jack admits. "A few cabins in the sparse woods, owned by those who don't want company."

"I see." But I don't see. I wonder if alligators stick to one brushy piece of shore, or if they like to venture out for a change of diet. Salty oiled tourists perhaps, done to a crisp and still warm from the sun. What respectable reptile could resist that? It is after all, not that far of a swim to the tourist beaches full of rafts, snorkeling, and well, people hanging out in the water like human bait.

"It's not the kind of information we'd want to share," Jack informs us, with a raised eyebrow.

Ava nods her head and I just stare at Jack Conner. Who is this man, nearly legend at this point on the island for his millions of dollars and secret dealings, his parade of insecure girlfriends who fall hopelessly in love with his wit and charm, and then run when his charisma turns into sarcastic criticism? Rumors fly everywhere with tales of drug money and weapons exchanging hands for a price.

Is any of it true?

Does Mr. Nash have people's heads smashed by coconut weaponry when they cross him? I prefer to think these charming maverick men are merely good targets for island gossip.

The bar has emptied of most patrons and only a few hardy locals remain. Ava and I discuss the difficulties of getting a taxi at two a.m. Without a word Jack walks over to the bartender, setting us up with two motor scooters for the trip home, and the rest of the week. They are the most popular form of transportation on the island. Jack obviously knows the bartender quite well, and that he rents the scooters lined up on the beach to tourists. It is also obvious Jack isn't ready to call it a night.

On the way home we dodge what we think is a land crab in the road, but upon closer examination, it is a tarantula. Ava shines her headlight on it, and I realize just how big our furry friend is. During the night I awaken several times trying to brush a huge hairy black spider out of my dreams.

At five thirty a.m. I am on the deck again and the ocean is the same, calm as ever. A constant, gentle current pulls it to the left. There are no waves because a reef surrounds the island, and acts as a buffer. The reef makes for some of the best diving in the world. Roatan is featured in all the magazines that list best dive locations. I wonder if any of those divers or dive magazines know about the alligator on the north shore.

While typing on my laptop midmorning a pack of wild dogs howl at something in the distance. A cat slinks through the yard. It would seem all pets here are more wild than tame unless you capture them at birth and confine them the way Ava has confined her kitty, Tommy Jean (named after the famous jeans designer, Tommy Hilfiger, whose third world counterfeit copies are popular on the island).

Tommy is hanging out with me on the deck. She likes to bat at palm leaves scraping against the wooden planks, and stares attentively at birds in nearby trees. She pounces on butterflies in flowering bushes but never seems to catch any.

By eleven a.m. Ava and I are off to the east shore on our scooters and excited about snorkeling, despite our new information about gnarly creatures possibly living on the north bank. The crystal clear water allows spectacular visibility. A three-foot barracuda hovers in the distance while tiny purple-and-blue fish swim beneath me. There are larger varieties in bright pink. A school of yellow-and-black striped tropical fish, with their round bodies and puckered lips, gaze at me curiously. It is a wonderland beneath the sea. The reef, only yards offshore, is perfect for lazy day snorkelers (like me) who don't want to swim out far.

"Should we quit before the sharks and gators come looking for lunch?" Ava shouts at me from across the water.

"Yes, I think we should go looking for lunch ourselves!" I shout back.

Swimming to shore we dry off in the sun and ride the scooters home, where we chop up garden tomatoes with fresh cilantro, and avocados off the tree next door. We heat up black beans cooked earlier and Ava warms her homemade tortillas to wrap everything in. I slice mangoes picked on the property and make a fruit salad by adding a few of Miss Alene's hook-ripened bananas and some shaved coconut.

"Don't you ever buy canned goods or prepackaged foods?" I ask.

"No," Ava tells me. "Canned goods on the island are an unnecessary extravagance. Everyone here grows or buys fresh produce and cooks from scratch. There is no need for convenience food on laid-back island time." She winks at me.

"I saw your pantry. There's Campbell's soup in there and Aunt Jemima pancake mix." I shoot her a mom look.

"Okay, well, we do make exceptions." Ava laughs.

In the late afternoon we catch a water taxi down the shoreline and buy supplies at the general store tucked away on its own beach with an adjacent bar and boat rentals. Two tall, lean natives man the water taxi, and when we arrive at the general store another willowy native approaches them. I watch the little huddle of these skinny dark men exchange packages as Ava and I wait to exit the sleek water ferry.

"What are they doing?" I whisper.

Ava glances their way and then gives me a sober look. "Mom, don't watch them. They're exchanging drugs for money. It happens all the time on the water taxi."

We stand to exit and Ava points to the gorgeous beach and picturesque palms. "Let's grab a sandwich from the store and sit by the shore to eat our lunch," she says, a little on the loud side considering I am standing right next to her. I take the hint and ignore the huddle of dark men, whose bare backs glisten in the hot afternoon sun.

Once in the general market I ask Ava a about them as we comb the old wooden shelves for reasonably priced staples to take back to the house. "What kind of drugs were they selling?" I whisper.

"Cocaine, generally, although I didn't see the white powder but I have in the past."

"Is that the most popular drug here?"

"Yes, if you can afford it. If not, all the regular cheaper fare is also plentiful."

I think about how this tiny island with all its majestic beauty is tainted by drugs, prejudice, and poverty. For every brilliant tropical fish in the colorful reef below the sea, a tarantula crawls along the forest belly. Ava has told me about the law in Roatan. If two people didn't see it happen, there was no crime. Even murder is ignored without witnesses willing to testify. Nowhere in the world does peace and harmony abound, but this picture postcard island borders on anarchy and I am frightened for Ava.

On our scooter ride home we pass Spanish-speaking natives selling produce from the back of their pickup. Ava and I stop to purchase a small, round, locally grown watermelon (sandia), and island oranges (narranjas), which are sweet, juicy, and green-skinned. We also pick out a big ripe pineapple (pina) and get limes (limons) to make margaritas. The best part is listening to Ava barter with the natives in Spanish.

When we return to the house, we make a pasta dish and eat it with the Chilean wine purchased in town. It is an excellent wine and I decide to ship some home. Lazily we finish the bottle on the deck feeling like island kings. We watch geckos snatch bugs from around the porch lights and play rummy with an old deck of cards while listening to The Rolling Stones on a portable stereo until late into the night. I tell Ava about my fears for her here and she nods, but soon the wine and the music lighten our mood and we share a few laughs about Jack and Mr. Nash, head smashing coconuts, unsavory reptiles, and tarantulas the size of land crabs.

I sleep like a baby on the Chilean wine, lulled to dreamland by the monstrous window machine that blows cool air over my sunburned and muscle-aching body, both evidence of my having a true island adventure.

The next day a storm is brewing, and takes all morning to slowly build. I have decided the tarantula seen crossing the road in the dead of night was an omen. Clouds have covered the horizon in puffy formations. In the distance, an ominous color begins to move our way. We sit on the porch eating our fresh fruit bought at the market yesterday and watch the agitated water around the dock in the sea by our rented cottage. Wind moves precariously through the banana leaves and grape trees. By now the sky is dark and the humid air is thicker than ever. Not a bird or lizard is stirring. A strange silence precedes the downpour.

Falling hard and fast the rain refreshes everything it touches, and replenishes the water supply for many who rely on roof gutters to fill their cisterns. Thunder and lightning give a thrill but not a threat, for both are high and distant rather than low and near. Ava tells me how sometimes the rain falls so fast you can't see the ocean, accompanied by thunder and lightning to equal its furry.

We wait out the storm by doing laundry in Ava's new machine, hooked up to the backside of the wraparound porch. I have a perfect view of the garden while sorting colors. The machine is compliments of Ava's landlord, Miss Alene. Ava grins and claims she has a "solar dryer" to go with the new machine. Handing me a basket of wooden clothespins, we clip our wet laundry on a line stretched across the porch. She shows me how to make her homemade flour tortillas while our clothes billow in the wind. After learning to appreciate the art of stretching dough into a flat six-inch round cake for frying, I am eager to stuff them with beans and rice for our lunch.

The rain has subsided as we eat our tortillas on the porch, and the Spanish-speaking gardener has meandered out to groom the grounds on Miss Alene's property. He shouts *Buenos Dias* to us. Ava says the same thing back. There is no evidence, when looking skyward, that it rained like cats and dogs earlier. The hard dirt streets and walkways on the other hand, have become muddy and speckled with puddles.

Not wanting to ride the scooters on muddy streets, we walk past the Internet Café and down the gravel road to catch a taxi into West End for the afternoon. Once there we buy counterfeit Ray-Bans for ten dollars from a street vendor who sells them to cruise ship patrons, docked here for the day. We stay for happy hour at a bar on the strip beside the beach and drink our personal favorite Honduran brew, called Salva Vida. Salva "save," and Vida "life."

Our next day is spent reading the latest paperback thrillers on the dock in front of Ava's house. We pick warm tomatoes and peppers from the garden for making salsa and squeeze the limes for an afternoon snack of nachos and margaritas. The roads are baked hard from the sun once again and we decide to look for evening adventure.

Ava and I ride the scooters to an exquisite French restaurant on the strip in West End. It is an oddity to find this oasis of sophistication in West End. Until now I thought only West Bay, where the sand is raked and Italians go topless, offered such elegance. The restaurant has a twenty-five-foot open-beam ceiling of island-grown mahogany, and is open on the ocean side. Three green-and-red macaws eye us from their wire cage in the corner, next to a festive red Coca-Cola machine looking more exotic than the birds for being foreign to this environment.

I soon spy an ocean view through serrated leaves shooting out from short sturdy pear palms, named for the shape of their trunks. They surround the restaurant, and grow profusely throughout the island, harboring their coconut fruit in smooth yellow or green husks. While enjoying sweet delights and fine liquor at this table with a partial view, Jack Conner shows up.

After hugs all around we insist he join us and Jack soon has a heavy tale to share of local news. "One of our crew members got himself shot last night," he tells us, downing a shot of tequila from the bottle already delivered to our table by doting staff, who obviously know Jack well.

"Who?" Ava asks.

"Not anyone you'd know," Jack answers. "Just a less reliable native we used occasionally when shorthanded. He was a user and I don't hire druggies full time. Probably owed more money to the dealers than he could come up with fast enough."

"Was anyone arrested?" I asked, but I could guess the answer.

"No." Jack downed another shot. People are murdered on this island all the time and I've never seen anyone arrested yet. It's usually about drugs. Sometimes it's about cheating wives." Jack smiles. "Not much else worth murdering for here in Roatan, except maybe property rights."

I take a long look at Jack Conner and wonder how many categories fit him for murder. The drug selling rumors are probably false. Jack's too smart for that, and has no reason to get involved with drug trafficking that I can tell. He already has more money than the drug runners have dreamt of. Now cheating wives is a real possibility. Mr. Connor could charm the pants off anyone looking for a south sea adventure. As for angering others over property rights, that's a slam-dunk. I wonder if he sleeps with a gun under his pillow.

We talk for hours at the table by the pear palm, Ava and I drinking tall exotic drinks with umbrellas and straws, Jack downing shots from his expensive upper shelf tequila. I am completely caught up in his sailing stories, for this man has earned his vivid tales through gutsy living in his youth, as a licensed captain for deep sea fishing expeditions. He speaks of swells higher than the boat he's in, on a pitch-black night in the middle of an ocean that isn't cooperating for reaching shore. I can see Jack Connor at the helm of the boat, ocean spray in his sandy hair, a determined look in his steel blue eyes.

It's an image hard to shake. Somehow I don't think Jack will meet his demise in the ocean he has sported a love affair with his entire life. No, something much less romantic will be his end, something ugly and small and probably avoidable, were he to care at all about the thoughts of others.

As our evening concludes I try not to consider that tomorrow is my last day in Roatan. In bed I fitfully dream of storms on the sea outside Ava's door, with monstrous swells that roll in like a wall of death. I want to pack a suitcase for Ava and bring her home like a petulant child needing parental supervision. But the steady hum of the window machine reminds me there is order here somewhere in the chaos, and a need to find one's own way in the world. We can't coddle our children forever, especially not when we've raised them to be strong, independent thinkers.

My last morning in Roatan Ava and I visit Coexen Hole. It is where the islanders do business and buy necessary supplies. There is one main roadway filled with bartering people and crazy unstructured traffic. Glaring poverty is only yards behind connected wooden storefronts. Some of the shops house special treasures such as hand-carved mahogany trunks and black island pottery, made in the exact same way for many generations.

I carefully examine every exquisite piece of carved wood and shaped pottery, picking my mementos wisely, as if they will have the burden of housing my memories made here for a lifetime.

Ava and I head to West End later for a Saturday night of celebrating my great adventure on the island. We splurge and use precious gas, taking the four-wheel-drive pickup to a local resort called Laguna Beach. It is just a jaunt down the dirt road beside the shoreline in front of Ava's house. When we arrive the music is loud in the cozy bar with a wooden dance floor. Drinks are strong and flow generously among the crowd that has gathered for some Saturday night action. It is a fine way to end my vacation in Roatan. American military men stationed in Honduras are at the bar, and divers from Europe, Australia, Canada, and the States. It's a friendly mix of locals and tourists alike.

Ava and I find an empty table for two tucked back by the wall and sadly speak of my trip ending. Even this festive dance hall cannot lighten our heaviness of heart.

"Ava, you need to be really careful, especially where the business is concerned. I don't think you should ever consider delivering money to the building site again."

"I won't, Mom. I know this island and how to look out for myself. I promise." She gives me a reassuring smile.

"It couldn't hurt to distance yourself a little from Jack. He doesn't seem to be well liked by anyone except those whose liquor he buys."

Ava laughs. "No one is holding me responsible for the decisions of Jack Conner."

I want to believe her. I want to think all the Thomas Nash's on the island would never harm a hair on her head with their arsenal of coconuts. I want to think hurricane Mitch will never have a brother swim up to shore here. I wish to believe the drug runners on the water taxis who look at her with pure lust in their eyes won't come looking for my Ava on a dark night. Mainly, I want to stop thinking like a protective mother, because it is draining my courage to leave her here with only Max for protection from wild packs of dogs and a jungle of hairy spiders.

Determined to enjoy our last night together we head to the dance floor and move with the lively music. We meet people, make fleeting friends and down a few more rum-and-Cokes. Altogether the friendly environment lightens our mood.

While talking to everyone throughout the evening I find no matter their differences or reasons for being there, they all are of the belief that a better adventure could not be found anywhere. The tiny island of Roatan with its untamed shores and pristine sea somehow steals into your heart. Maybe it's the subtlety of danger lurking just beyond the beachfront palms, or the tranquility of an ocean with no pounding surf. Much like a forbidden lover, Roatan works its way into your soul and holds you on an edge of fear mixed with stolen moments by an emerald sea . . . and I shall treasure every one of mine.

After many hugs and tears, and promises of return trips I leave for the States. Alligators on the north shore fade into the recesses of my mind as I maneuver through customs back home. It isn't until I unwrap my mementos bought in Coexen Hole on my last day that I recollect all my concerns, and marvel at my exotic memories.

Five years after my final trip to Roatan my daughter's father-in-law was murdered in cold blood on the island. He was shot multiple times in the head. It happened late at night while checking on his boat. Nothing had been disturbed and there were no witnesses. It is a cautionary tale for those seeking shores of white sand already claimed by natives who preceded them on the island . . . perhaps disputably so, but argumentatively fair.

for want of love

is there a time
when hearts rejoice
and sing a melody
that outshines the stars?

or are we destined
to reach beyond
the boundaries of space
and find no trace of
happiness or meaning?

what is this thing
called life, where
those that look
for more, end up with less
except for suffering?
were we meant to
be content as shells
empty, longing,
alone?

there are no winners,
only those who know
nothing about
such battles of the soul.
and then there are those
who reap the spoils

of another's sacrifice
for want of a love
that is not theirs . . .

to give, or take.

benjamin

Rafting the Rogue was Rachel's idea. I could see her lean tomboyish form smiling at me from the trail above the river, shouting a greeting not distinguishable over the roaring water. I watched her tanned figure scrambling down the embankment, short honey-colored hair hugging her face. Rachel Milan had been my best friend since high school. I would always associate meeting her with the devastating event of my mother's death. The Milan family had moved into the house next door and Rachel became an angel of mercy in the presence of despair. She made me laugh again, and made grief tolerable.

The men who would join our rafting group soon arrived in an old Ford pickup. They parked it beside Rachel's dusty convertible at the top of the embankment. I could hear their baritone voices above the rushing river as they hauled sleeping bags and backpacks to the shuttle van.

The whitewater company provided tents, prepared meals, and promised numerous whitewater thrills. They also provided our expert guides, Eric and Martin. I had grown up hiking and camping in the lush Oregon woods and was excited about this new adventure. Still, I couldn't help but wonder if it would be more of a thrill than any of us had bargained for, none of us having rafted a wild river before. If nothing else, it would be a testament to our courage, to stay the course for three long days.

Rachel finally reached where I stood, and we embraced in a welcoming hug. We curiously viewed the men who would be joining us.

"Do you know their names?" I asked.

Rachel observed them thoughtfully. "The blond is Daniel Rosselli. Jonathan is the tall dark-haired one beside him. His parents are friends of Miranda's in New York."

"Where is Miranda?" I asked, but Rachel wasn't listening. Her cat-green eyes were focused on the strong current, watching it move downstream to a wide bend in the river. The dry forest gave off a scent of pine needles and wood bark as the morning quickly heated up and I pulled my heavy hair into a ponytail.

Miranda finally arrived and we added her gear to the shuttle van while listening to her tale of taking a wrong exit off the freeway. It was wonderful to see her. Miranda Tanasborne was tall and willowy with exotic features and a soul-warming laugh. I had missed her terribly since moving out of our apartment in the spring, having graduated with a doctorate in psychology.

It was Miranda and her friend Jonathan who had put the trip together. She introduced Robert as Jonathan's law partner, and said Daniel was working on a doctorate in religious studies. It was hard not to stare at Daniel. He had flaxen hair that fell nearly to his shoulders in thick waves. His eyes were some exotic shade of tropical blue, not typical for humans. Cyan to be exact, a primary color used for blending cool tones when painting. All three men looked quite capable of masterfully rafting the wild river, and I was thankful for that.

Eric was the guide who sat at the head of our lightweight raft. He was an excellent coach and we took to it quickly, rowing in unison while making good time all morning. Martin, our other guide, manned the supply boat following well behind us. The day was cloudless and bright, the Rogue peaceful and calm on this beginning section of our rafting trip. We were a pride-filled team of somewhat weary rowers when pulling onto a sandbar for lunch. Everyone reapplied sunscreen and wolfed down roast beef sandwiches, anticipating the thrill of a class-four rapid later in the day. Already such expert rowers, surely we would slide easily through.

The first section of river after lunch was exceptionally still, being protected by cliffs on either side. At one point we jumped from the raft and floated through a sheer rock canyon. The chilly water was a welcome relief from the hot sun. Our laughter bounced off canyon walls as we slid through with only our life vests to keep us afloat. Eric wasn't far behind, sitting at the helm of the otherwise empty raft. Martin could be seen in the far off distance with the supply boat.

Floating on our backs we all admired the intense blue sky above the sheer rock walls. I tried to focus on a hawk gliding through the air with his outstretched wings soaring far above me. At the end of the canyon we approached a narrow beach. Pulling ourselves out of the chilly river, we all lay on the sandbar until dried out and warmed up by the sun. It wasn't long until Eric announced it was time to end the calm before the storm.

Rested from our swim through the canyon, we were eager to face the class-four rapid. I positioned myself behind Daniel in the raft and listened intently to our guides describe the tricky rowing task ahead. My companions were all quiet as they absorbed their instructions. We looked at one another with confidence before taking off from the shallow beach and heading downstream to our greatest challenge of the trip.

Just as Martin and Eric predicted, our entrance into the shallows before the swirling drop-off steered us sharply to the right. We rowed forcefully to position ourselves correctly for this ride through the fast approaching, tumultuous rapid. But the raft didn't swing back to the left as we hoped it would. Despite our coordinated rowing, we were trapped in the swirling middle. Maybe it was too much adrenalin among us, but despite our synchronized effort we remained dead center, being jerked continually about for what seemed like an eternity. Working diligently to pull ourselves free, first with one side rowing hard and deep, and then the other, we at last broke loose.

Darting quickly from the center of the rapid the rubberized boat tilted out of control. I saw fear in Rachel's eyes across from me and then heard Miranda scream from behind. As if suspended in time I felt the boat flip and toss me high into the air. I inhaled deeply on the way down instinctively knowing I'd be swallowed by the river, and swallowed I was—plunging downward into the bowels of the Rogue.

Wedged beneath rapidly moving water I felt helpless to stop myself from being pummeled by tons of flowing river. How long could I hold my breath? Panic set in and I began fighting my way back to the surface. Surely my lungs would burst before I freed myself. I struggled to remove the life jacket. It was only a deterrent to me now, its buoyancy useless while stuck beneath the strong currents.

For an instant I quit struggling and stared through blurry wetness, my heart beating fast and hard while being held hostage there. Time was of the essence. Had I considered every alternative for resurfacing? Fear of inhaling this bubbly aqua beast that gripped me caused one last gallant effort to break free. Kicking ferociously to rise above the strong current and be among the living left no time for profound thoughts as I quickly ran out of breath. I only regretted my weak slender build. There was no light miraculously appearing except for the sun teasing me from above as I thrashed upwards.

Still my efforts weren't enough. My lungs were burning painfully. I was seconds from inhaling the river and meeting my maker. I hated dying this way. I hated dying at all. I wanted to live. I still had so much living to do. Something gripped my upper arm then, I was sure of it . . . or was it a cramp? Was it God pulling me to heaven? Something was yanking me upwards.

I was suddenly pulled clear from the suffocating river and instantly felt lighter. No sooner had the air hit my face than I sucked in a lungful of it, nearly choking to death as I exhaled, while being deposited on a rock. It was only after clearing my eyes and throat that I dared glimpse who or what had pulled me free from the Rogue.

It was Daniel. Seeing that I was okay he lay down on the rock beside me. I couldn't speak at first. The sun was glaring from above and I was aware of sharp sounds, not muffled like beneath the water. The river rushing past made a thunderous roar and moved completely through me, like an orchestra of percussion instruments pounding on my chest. Birds were chirping in the trees on the shore. I squinted through my hair, plastered to my face on either side, and realized Daniel and I were in the center of the Rogue, on a large flat rock.

"Where are the rest?" I whispered hoarsely.

"They . . . grabbed the raft," Daniel answered, breathing heavily. "They're fine, I think. Back a quarter mile . . . or so, I'm guessing."

He sat up and I could see the silhouette of his strong body against the sun. Thank God he was there when I needed him, this angel of a man, who actually looked the part.

"We shot down the river much faster underwater . . . than they did on top of it . . . clinging to the raft," he added tentatively, as if it were a theory he'd come up with and only hoped it were true. So did I. Surely we were the only two who nearly drowned.

I shivered violently despite the hot sun beating down onto my limp flesh and suddenly was grateful Martin kept my camera on the supply boat. This rafting adventure was a short diversion from my graduate studies in graphic art. I was a photographer, and had bought an expensive waterproof camera for the trip. Pointless for it to be waterproof, if lying on the riverbed!

Sitting up slowly, I stared into Daniel's unusual blue eyes. They had such a calming effect. It didn't seem to matter anymore that we were on a rock in the middle of a wild river. I felt safe. I hoped our companions were safe too.

"Thanks, Daniel. For saving my life."

"You don't need to thank me, Tori." He studied my face and I wondered if my thoughts were transparent. We had shared something horrific and beaten the odds. Flipping was never supposed to happen and always a death threat when it did.

"I was just in the right place at the right time and did what anyone would do." He smiled at me. "But then again, I guess we were both in the wrong place at the wrong time." Daniel looked over his shoulder to see if the raft was coming.

Why did I agree to come on this trip? How had Rachel squelched my fears about rafting the unpredictable Rogue? I could hear her voice in my head. *There's really nothing to it. By the end of the second day you'll be wishing it would never end. It's going to be fun and the memories will get you through the rest of the summer, while doing all that filing for Professor Cairns.*

I watched noisy seagulls sail across the cloudless sky and then stared into the tons of river rushing by. The Rogue would end its journey at the Pacific Ocean, downstream in the little coastal town of Gold Beach. It had started out as a mountain stream, snow runoff trickling downhill. Where along the way to its destination had this lamb become a lion?

"Look." Daniel nodded and pointed toward the bend, where the raft full of our companions was drifting into view. They cheered when seeing us. Eric was in front skillfully maneuvering over to our rock, followed by Martin in the supply boat.

"I guess you're both 'like one' with the river now!" Eric boomed, looking visibly shaken despite his attempt at humor. Rachel and Miranda mauled me with hugs and tears as I climbed aboard the raft. Jonathan and Robert appeared sober and relieved, shaking Daniel's hand and patting him on the back. Once it became clear Daniel and I were not injured and only wished to press on toward camp for the night, we all began paddling in unison. It felt good to be rowing, to be alive, to be alone with my thoughts as we rounded the bend toward our stopping point for the first day.

Everyone was somber that last hour, breaking the methodical rhythm of our rowing only once, to point at snowy white egrets perched along the bank. Our private thoughts were surely all the same, trying to understand what had happened and what a close call it was. The Rogue was indeed a force to be reckoned with. In certain places it became tranquil and serene, but for the most part it was exuberant, challenging, and worthy of respect. I thought of it now as something more than just thrilling. It was threatening, if circumstance permitted.

Campfire conversation sizzled with stories of the spill while we devoured Eric's pan-fried salmon and wild rice, suddenly starving from hard rowing and emotional trauma. Someone began a conversation about colleges and occupations. Rachel and I shared how college swept us away from the small Oregon towns of our youth, making us city dwellers now, in Portland proper. Miranda lived in Portland too, although originally from New York like Jonathan and Robert. She had come for graduate school and fell in love with *The City of Roses*. Jonathan and Robert practiced law in Portland, having been enticed equally by deep-sea fishing in small northwest coastal towns and a law firm offering immediate partnership. Daniel studied religion in Portland. No one said how he'd met Jonathan and Robert.

What other great adventures would we have during our time on the river, before pulling out at Foster Bar on the last day? We were at least grateful there were no more class-four rapids. Jonathan began poking the fire with a tree branch. He stopped for a minute to look directly at me. "Tori is an odd name. Is it short for something?"

"It's short for Victoria. Tori is found conveniently in the middle," I explained. "The nickname eliminates expectation that I will be victorious in whatever I attempt."

"I would say not drowning was quite victorious." Jonathan smiled. Rachel and Miranda agreed appreciatively.

"I would have drowned, were it not for Daniel plucking me from the river," I pointed out.

"Well, your eyes are intimidating." Jonathan stared at me. "They are quite bold and a striking shade of blue. Very powerful, like your name." Until that moment I'd always believed my large eyes overwhelmed my face. That they came across as powerful was thought provoking. Power eluded me to be sure, like my name, perhaps powerful in the longer form but a quandary in its shortened version. I didn't know the longer version of myself yet, the one that could go the distance.

I fell silent, not knowing what to say in response, but I liked Jonathan. His smile was infectious. He had a sharp wit that kept everyone laughing, and he rowed with more finesse than any of us.

At some point Daniel and I began to quietly observe each other from across the fire. It was unclear to me what I thought of this odd man. We had nothing in common but nearly drowning, and out-of-the-ordinary eye color. Yet his affect on me was profound. It didn't feel flirtatious, like with Jonathan. It felt more spiritual, if such a word could be in my vocabulary. We knew more than anyone how close we'd come to death and how lucky we were to be alive. We shared what the point of no return feels like, just before it miraculously turns because of unbelievable good fortune, or maybe divine intervention.

After everyone crawled into sleeping bags placed in tents put up earlier, I quietly grabbed my sweatshirt and crept down to the shoreline. I couldn't sleep. Almost drowning had my head swimming with thoughts of my mother, who was killed instantly when her car slid off an icy mountain road and over an embankment. I was fourteen at the time. My father would have found the news of my death an intrusion into his new life, a rude reminder of his former marriage and first kids. Did my sister Eliza regret our drifting apart after Mother died? Eliza left for college right after the funeral but Wil and I became close while living with Grams during high school. Surely we could have made more effort to call and visit these past few years.

I was staring at the star-cluttered sky, trying to shake off these troubling thoughts when Daniel startled me, jumping onto the boulder from behind. I gasped and then relaxed. Here we were on a rock once again. Only this one overlooked the river from the shore, rather than being wedged in the middle of the Rogue.

Almost drowning fine-tuned my senses. The water sounded magnified as it rushed by, and moonlight danced on the surface with intense sparks of light. I keenly felt the heat of the sun still trapped inside the boulder beneath us. Even my sense of touch was ultra-sensitive as his arm brushed mine.

"Couldn't you sleep either?"

"No," he confessed.

The scent of bar soap mixed with wood smoke on his skin was enticing and intoxicating all at the same time. Daniel must have found me somewhat irresistible as well, because he slowly reached out to touch my face, running his fingers along my cheek bone. Finally he drew me near and kissed my forehead. It sent a chill straight through me. Had it not been such a strange day I would have found it odd, getting chills from a kiss on the forehead. The full moon was literally making Daniel's golden locks shimmer. I'd wanted to touch them ever since being stranded on a rock in the river. The hot sun had dried his hair quickly, illuminating the flaxen curls as if he were not entirely of this world, but half hovering in another.

Now in the moonlight I could finally run my fingers through his blond tresses, recalling that moment of sheer gratitude for being rescued. Daniel pulled me closer and kissed my mouth. It made my heart race out of control and reminded me of floating through the air earlier, before hitting the water. Like a dam breaking, there was no stopping this floodgate of feelings pouring out of us. Nestled in soft foliage beside the rock we intermingled silent thought and sensual touch until we dare not stay another minute. While sneaking back to our cold and empty sleeping bags, I hoped no one would be the wiser for how and where we'd spent the night.

At daybreak our two guides could be heard cracking branches for kindling. The sun was barely rising above evergreens on the far shore when they began brewing coffee, enticing us from our tents. I was the first to sit by the welcoming flames licking at freshly split wood. Jonathan soon approached us and began asking Eric questions about what type of whitewater thrills we could expect for the day. Eric laughed and assured him there'd be no more class-four rapids.

At breakfast we sat on opposite ends of a fallen tree, drinking strong coffee and inhaling biscuits smothered in gravy. None of our companions sandwiched between us seemed to have noticed our absence from the tents, much to our relief.

Everyone was eager to break camp after breakfast and begin our journey down the river, but I managed to take some impressive shots with my new camera. The early morning sun was already warm and bright as it filtered through Douglas fir trees and danced on the surface of the water. Boldly standing on a rock at the river's edge was breathtaking. It was quite beautiful with sunlight glistening on each little eddy.

Daniel rowed directly in front of me all morning, and I in front of him all afternoon. Memories of lovemaking beside the river made not touching him in the raft difficult. I had no indication as to whether or not it was equally difficult for Daniel, because we barely acknowledged each other's presence until breaking for lunch.

While our companions dangled their feet in the water and savored more roast beef sandwiches, we crawled onto a tall rock formation to be alone. I snapped a few pictures from our perch above the river and told Daniel everything he didn't know about photography. He shared the history and teachings of Christianity. It was intriguing to me how he didn't preach the message of the gospel I'd heard so often as a child. Instead he offered up the most fascinating little known facts about the early Church of Rome.

After lunch, we received curious smiles from our friends, except for Jonathan, who wasn't smiling at all. For the next two days Daniel and I were inseparable, but discreet. Never openly affectionate, never alluding to what became our continual nighttime gathering by the river's edge, where I chose to place my sleeping bag, and where Daniel always came to lie beside me. The intensity of our lovemaking left us sweaty and spent, finally dozing in each other's arms until nearly dawn. It felt as if our very souls were becoming as entangled as our flesh.

Then all too soon it was time to return to civilization.

Our parting breakfast was quite sober. Daniel and I, along with our companions, reminisced about everything we'd experienced. What Daniel and I experienced alone only our eyes disclosed between us. When the rafts drifted slowly past the last bend in the channel at mid-morning, I could barely believe our magical time in the wilderness was coming to an end. The water and trees became a blur to me as they passed by. It was as if they were an illusion. But upon reflection, perhaps the river and forest were the only things exactly as they seemed.

At the pullout sight I awkwardly said my last goodbye to Rachel and Miranda, still refusing to share my feelings about Daniel. I felt discussing our affair would make it perfectly clear to me what an absolute crazy thing I'd done, throwing caution to the wind, along with better judgment. I didn't usually fall into relationships as easily as pinecones off a tree, nor would I normally give my heart to someone I barely knew. I didn't wish to examine what exactly happened between Daniel and me. Perhaps the river I nearly succumbed to affected my sanity.

I rearranged the gear in my trunk, and waited for Daniel to say goodbye to me alone. Jonathan and Robert were talking with the guides, obviously waiting for him to see me off. Finally Daniel approached my car. We hugged briefly.

"Will I ever hear from you again?" I asked.

"Of course."

He didn't sound convincing. I'd given Daniel my e-mail address, but he hadn't offered me his, and I had too much pride to ask for it. "Daniel, is there someone else . . . was this time together meant to be forgotten?"

"No, there's not anyone else . . . there's never been anyone else." Daniel stared into the cloudless sky. "I have never felt this way before. I should not have allowed myself . . ." his voice trailed off.

"Are you afraid I'll interfere with your studies?"

"That's not it." He glanced at Jonathan and Robert.

"What then?" I also glanced at them, recalling my conversation with Jonathan on that first night. It seemed so long ago. He saw me looking his way and we held eye contact for several seconds.

I tried to ignore Jonathan's disapproving stare while examining Daniel's odd expression. He was somber, brows knit—no smile. It was as if his mind were somewhere far away and yet intensely focused on the moment. "I love you, Tori. I've never said that to anyone." He looked at me one last time and then walked away.

I got into my car and left, thinking about how I was almost taken by the river only to be transformed by it instead. Yet there was no joy in my heart about it, no peace of mind or excited anticipation. What if Daniel never contacted me? I felt a knot forming in the pit of my stomach as I sped down the hard dirt road. But of course he would. I shrugged off my fear of never seeing him again as I left the Oregon wilderness behind. What I couldn't shrug off was the expression on Daniel's face as he had said goodbye.

It was a look of such total remorse.

"He has a gift . . . your Benjamin."

Benjamin let go of the sparrow and it faltered for a second as we held our breath, but then flapped its wings and flew away into the blue sky. The little bird made a sharp turn and was soon out of sight. We both jumped up and down on the patio while clapping our hands, relieved and happy.

"That's the second bird this month you've nursed back to health, Benjamin." I hugged my little golden-haired son and ran fingers through his messy curls. "I'm proud of you, Benj," I added, kissing him on the cheek before walking back inside the apartment.

I leaned against the kitchen counter with my steaming mug of tea and observed Benjamin peering off into the sky, his sick pet healed and gone. At eleven years old he was bringing home wounded animals and nursing them back to health, and had been ever since he turned five. He always fell in love with his little pets, and yet he never kept any. Once they were healed he promptly released them back into the wilds of the city.

Benjamin was such a sweet boy, beautiful and smart. His eyes were some exotic shade of blue seen only in the shallow waters of a warm, tropical ocean. They were cyan blue, to be exact, the same shade as Daniel's, with the same dancing slivers of light, and they were always full of questions. Questions he never asked, such as who was his father? Why wasn't he part of our lives?

Maybe it was just my own guilt putting the questions there. Maybe his inquisitive expression only reflected his innocence, his pure heart. And he did have a pure heart. Benjamin was extraordinary. He never cried as a baby, or rebelled as a toddler. He never hit or yelled, or lost his patience. Animals loved him. Everyone in the neighborhood loved Benjamin—big kids, little kids, adults. It didn't matter what their ethnic diversity was—and we had a plethora of cultures and colors on our street. They all saw something in him they admired and respected, something they wanted to protect.

Sitting down at my computer and checking the gallery website again, I realized it wouldn't be long until we could move out of the inner city. I could buy us a real home with a big yard and Benjamin could go to the good schools in the suburbs. I'd finally sold enough Gallery photos for a down payment. Becoming pregnant on the Rogue trip set back my graduate program, but I hung in there, transferring to Portland State and taking classes at night. Now all my persistence and dedication was beginning to earn a decent income from sales at Rachel's art gallery.

Next to Benjamin's school picture was our only family photo. I must have been about eleven, the same age Benjamin was now. My father was quite handsome in the picture, and smiling. I couldn't remember him ever being that skinny, or smiling for that matter. Mother looked demure standing there beside him wearing a tight stylish dress, with her long dark hair twisted up and back.

If only my mother could see what I had accomplished. It was my one resounding and impossible wish. She had been the center of my universe as a child, but I was never the center of hers. Being the middle child with classic middle child syndrome by second grade, I appropriately and purposefully chose to go by the middle of my name. I believed in my child's heart *victory* had not been mine when it came to winning the affection of either parent. I was not as studious as my older sibling Eliza, or as entertaining as our little brother Wil. My only distinction came from inheriting our mother's creative gifts, and that didn't appear to be held in reverence like perfect grades or making people laugh.

My mother was just coming into her own as a renowned sculptor when her car slid off that icy mountain road in the Cascades. I often thought about how few seconds it takes to lose control on a mountain road and not be able to brake in time, or to plunge beneath the Rogue and not be able to resurface in time. She needed a savior that day, a Daniel to steer her to safety, to grab her and wrench her free from death's grip.

I touched the silver frame of Benjamin's school picture, moving my finger up to his cyan blue eyes and the curly golden hair, stopping at the soft yellow glow above his head. Photos of him always reflected light above his yellow-white hair. It wasn't just the hair and eyes that made Benjamin an oddity. It was his ability to heal things. That special gift must have come from Daniel. Why had he never called after the Rogue trip? I had asked myself this question many times, just as I continually recalled every precious moment of our short time together. Despite the endless heartache and unanswered questions for all these years, I thanked God that at least I had our son. Benjamin was a very special parting gift indeed.

There was a knock on the door and Benjamin came in from the patio to answer it. "Hello, Mrs. Gianni."

"Hi, Benji boy. You're just the person I want to see."

"Come in, Maggie, please." I stood from my desk.

"I'm sorry to bother you, but it's my Sarah." Maggie's voice broke and her eyes were puffy from crying.

"Sit down, Maggie. Tell us how Sarah's doing." I led her to the blue sofa with swirling flowers in faded yellows and sat next to her. Benjamin closed the door and perched on the edge of a matching chair. It had been Grams' furniture, worn with age but sturdy and soft, just as she had been.

"Sarah's bad, Tori. Really bad." Maggie unwadded the lace-trimmed hanky in her hand and dabbed at her eyes. She looked older than her forty-five years. Maybe it was the graying hair she pulled back into a tight bun, or all the worry that came with their daughter's cancer. Maggie and Vincent were more surprised than anyone when she became pregnant, after they'd given up. Sarah was their whole world, a petite and sensitive child with soft green eyes and hair the color of light molasses.

"I'm so sorry, Maggie. Is there anything we can do?" I glanced over at Benjamin. We both knew Sarah had cancer. Now a related infection was causing her to spike a high fever. The doctors sent her home from the hospital. There was nothing they could do. She would have to fight it out, or perhaps, quit fighting.

Maggie stuffed the hanky in a pocket of her green print blouse. She always wore loose fitting blouses with generous pockets on either side, carefully sewn on her Italian machine. I watched as she smoothed back a gray hair and looked past me onto the patio. Sunshine from the glass door fell in patches on the hardwood floor. No one spoke or moved as she composed herself.

"She's dying, Tori. I know it. She's slipping away and there's nothing I can do."

Benjamin came and sat on the other side of Maggie, setting one hand on her knee in comfort. I took her other hand and held it.

"She's asking for Benjamin." Maggie glanced at him and her eyes lit up. "She loves you, Benji. You're the best friend she's ever had. Will you come with me . . . now . . . to see her?"

Benjamin nodded and then looked at me. I smiled warmly at him. "He'd be happy to, Maggie. I pray you're wrong about her dying, and she breaks this fever," I whispered, squeezing her hand.

Maggie pulled the hanky back out of her pocket. "Come with us, honey." Her large brown eyes pleaded with me.

"Of course I will." Together we walked next door, with Benjamin trailing behind. Once in the Gianni's apartment, we timidly entered Sarah's room. Her father, Vincent, peered up at us with troubled eyes. I hugged his thin frame tightly and his eyes filled with tears as he whispered to me that his Sarah was dying. After patting Benjamin's messy golden curls, Vincent stepped out of the room for a much needed break.

Benjamin sat on the edge of Sarah's wrought-iron bed and looked calmly into her gaunt face. Maggie and I stood on the other side. I couldn't help but observe my son's undeniable peace with suffering.

What eleven-year-old would not be squirming by now or awkwardly fumbling with their hands or clothing? But Benjamin seemed to be comfortable with her near-death state. He took Sarah's pale hand into his and touched her hot cheek with the other. Instantly her eyes opened.

"*Benjamin.*" She whispered with finality, as if now everything would be tolerable. "I've missed you." There was the hint of a smile on her face.

"I've missed you, too, Sarah." He paused, carefully moving a stray hair off her forehead. "The sparrow flew away today. She's all healed."

Sarah's face lit up in response.

"You should've seen her, Sarah. She fell for a second and then flapped her wings wildly, fighting it, fighting the fall. Then she flew up . . . up really high . . ." Benjamin glanced out the window and Sarah turned her head to follow his gaze. ". . . made a sharp turn and was gone."

"I wish I could have been there," Sarah sighed.

Benjamin put his hand on her forehead. "You need to catch your fall, Sarah. Like the sparrow. Fight it."

Sarah stared into his eyes intently.

"You can do it, Sarah. Just fly up and away, well and strong."

Maggie caught more tears with her lace hanky and sniffled.

"Benj, we should go, honey. Sarah needs her rest," I said softly.

Benjamin glanced up at me and rose from the bed. He turned to look at her one last time. "Make a sharp turn, Sarah. Okay?"

"Okay, Benjamin." Sarah's green eyes sparkled, full of new strength.

I smiled at Sarah. She was only a year younger than Benjamin, but looked tiny in comparison. "Get well, sweetie. We miss you at our place." I kissed her forehead.

"She seems better, Maggie. Really," I whispered into her ear as I turned to go. "Please, call us if you need anything, anything at all. Okay?"

Maggie nodded, and I left, with Benjamin at my side.

Several weeks later I pulled cookies out of the oven and slid them onto a plate. "They're hot, Benj, be careful," I scolded while pouring us each a glass of milk.

"Mrs. Gianni told me Sarah's better." Benjamin took a bite of the warm chocolate cookie while sitting down at the solid oak table, compliments of Grams.

"Really? That's great, Benj. When did you see Maggie?" I sat across from him and set the glasses down.

"Just now. When I got home from school. She was getting the mail." He gulped down his milk and I gave him a thoughtful look.

"That doesn't mean Sarah's in remission, Benj. It just means her fever's gone because the infection healed."

"No." Benjamin shook his head. "She's in remission. Mrs. Gianni said so."

I set my cookie down and studied his angelic face. "Maggie said Sarah's in remission? Are you sure?"

"I'm sure." He looked at me seriously with his unbearably blue eyes. "Mrs. Gianni says she wants to return to school tomorrow. She wants me to walk with her."

"That's amazing, Benjamin. Really wonderful news." I looked through the patio window and thought about the sparrow, and about Sarah, both free falling to death for an instant, and then suddenly turning sharply away from it.

There was a knock on the door and Benjamin jumped up to see who was there. It was Maggie, grinning ear to ear. I stood to hug her as she cheerfully joined us at the table. We chatted happily about the good news. Benjamin promised to watch over Sarah at school her first day back. Then he left to do his homework and I insisted Maggie stay for a cup of tea.

"It was your Benjamin, Tori, who saved my Sarah. I know it was." Maggie swiped her eyes with a napkin as I set a cup of tea in front of her.

"Maggie, there's no way of knowing that," I said, but I believed my son *had indeed* healed the child. Maggie and I witnessed it together. Sarah's strength began to return the instant Benjamin touched her. The little girl's eyes went from bleary defeat to shimmering hope in a matter of seconds.

"He has a gift . . . your Benjamin. Like that Father Rosselli, at St. Matthew's."

"Father who?" I asked, dropping the sugar spoon and grabbing a napkin to blot tea splashes on the table.

"Father Rosselli. Everyone's heard of him. He's known for healing the sick, and the dying. Especially children." Maggie took a sip of tea.

"I was going to take my Sarah there tonight for his healing mass, but your boy beat him to it." Her whole face lit up from thinking about Sarah's miraculous remission. "They say he's going to be appointed bishop, because of his wonderful healings. The Pope himself is going to have a special ceremony for Father Rosselli, in Rome. This young priest, he comes from Rome originally," Maggie added.

I sat down and nodded my head, too perplexed by Maggie's information to speak.

"Have you heard of Father Rosselli, Tori?"

"No. I mean . . . I'm not sure." I put my hand on my forehead, suddenly feeling flushed. "What's his first name, Maggie? Do you know?" I gathered up the milk glasses and placed them in the sink.

Maggie stood and leaned against the counter. "I can't remember. I'm sorry." She paused. "Are you okay, honey?"

"I don't know. I need to see who this priest is. What time is the healing mass?" I looked into Maggie's questioning brown eyes.

"It's at five." She reached out and took my hands into hers. "Do you think you might know him?"

I took a deep breath. "Maybe. He might be someone from my college days. I'm just . . . surprised that he might be a priest."

Maggie indicated she understood and walked over to the door. "Goodbye, honey. I hope it's your friend. Maybe he can give you some insight into Benjamin's special gift for healing."

I considered the irony of my neighbor's words. Glancing at the stove clock I realized we could make the healing mass if we hurried. I shouted for Benjamin to come quickly while grabbing my purse and car keys. He followed me out the door, asking where we were going. I mumbled something about needing to sec someone I knew from a long time ago before he was born. Benjamin didn't ask any questions, and I was grateful, because I was thinking about questions of my own. For Father Rosselli. Could it be Daniel? Was this his mysterious occupation? Is that why he didn't call after our love affair on the Rogue?

Surely not, but I had to see for myself.

I honked my horn to avoid a near accident, and then glanced at Benjamin guiltily. His brows were knit with concern. Vowing to concentrate more carefully on traffic, I willed myself to stop the flood of emotions overtaking me. How often had I tried to examine what went wrong on the Rogue all those years ago? I believed the bond between Daniel and I was much more than physical. So much so that I agonized even now over why he didn't call, didn't look for me during all these years. Could it have been because he was a priest?

Cars honked and brakes squealed again. Benjamin jumped. "What is it, Mom? Are you okay?"

I glanced at him while chewing my bottom lip. "Benj, this mass we're going to, it's a healing mass."

"A healing mass?" Benjamin looked perplexed.

"Yeah. This Father . . . Rosselli, well, he heals people. Like you heal animals. And Maggie . . . Maggie thinks you healed Sarah." I glanced at him again, nervously.

Benjamin calmly asked, "Do we know him? Father Rosselli?"

"I'm not sure, Benj. But he's . . . like you, with the healing powers. So I want to see for myself."

Benjamin nodded, his flaxen hair moving slightly in the breeze from the window. I parked in the lot behind the Cathedral. Bells chimed as latecomers straggled up the cement steps to the arched doorway. I froze on the sidewalk and stared at the entrance. I could feel Benjamin hovering near my side and it gave me the presence of mind to continue, to follow through with finding out the truth. Was that Daniel in there? *Benjamin's father?*

Grabbing my son's hand I flew up the steps and through the entrance just as the ushers shut the massive oak doors. I let my eyes adjust to the dim light and then inched my way steadily forward until near the middle of the center aisle. Benjamin was right behind me. I genuflected and slipped inside the pew, kneeling as I made the sign of the cross, while Benjamin mirrored my actions perfectly.

After Mother died and I went to live with Grams, we attended St. Luke's every Sunday, missing only once when she was too ill. That Cathedral was small and humble in comparison, but the motions of a mass are exactly the same everywhere in the world. Benjamin and I prayed, sat back in the pew, and observed our ornate surroundings as inconspicuously as possible.

A tremendous pipe organ played a hymn and everyone stood to sing. The acolytes lit altar candles. Priests appeared from side alcoves. I strained to see them, wishing I'd had the nerve to sit up front in the enormous sanctuary. After everyone stopped singing and sat down, several laymen read verses from folded programs handed to worshipers on the way in. An older priest approached the wooden podium and read scripture from a large leather-bound Bible. Everyone stood reverently to listen.

My eyes never left the spacious and intricate altar area, watching every move made by the younger priest in black robes. I couldn't see his facial features well enough to determine if it was Daniel or not, but the height and build seemed right, and whoever it was, he had light hair. The older priest spoke intelligently, his words weighty and measured, but I couldn't concentrate. My mind raced uncontrollably to the past and then anxiously lingered in the present. Benjamin listened intently, his expression one of fascination, soaking up all that was happening like a sponge.

When it was time for communion my heart began pounding. I prayed for strength and took slow deep breaths as I entered the center aisle with Benjamin right in front of me. We followed the procession of worshipers until it was our turn for communion. I didn't have the courage to lift my head and look into the faces of the priests on the way up.

I felt weak and shaky, afraid if I did look at them I would surely faint.

Body of Christ, bread of heaven echoed in my ears as we approached the altar. Benjamin knelt in front of me and accepted the host into his mouth, just as everyone else had done. *Blood of Christ, cup of salvation.* He drank from the goblet, still mimicking other worshipers, then made the sign of the cross before circling back to our pew. I knelt and heard the words *body of Christ, bread of heaven,* and looked up into the face of Daniel, his cyan blue eyes showing immediate recognition. I felt a rush of warmth as he set the host on my tongue. Daniel's face drained of color and he wavered slightly, his golden hair shimmering under the lit candles as he caught his breath. *Blood of Christ, cup of salvation.* I drank from the goblet and then stood to face him.

Amen was all I could say in barely a whisper.

Tori emerged weakly from Daniel's lips.

For several seconds we stared into each other's eyes, and then I turned to leave, somehow finding my way back to the pew I had come from.

The rest of the mass was a blur of standing and singing, and special prayers said by Daniel for the sick. His voice was unsteady and trailed off several times, as if distracted from his purpose. Those who wished for hands-on healing approached and knelt at the altar and he touched them, whispering something over each one. After a while the pipe organ played and a final hymn was sung. People filed out of the church and I stayed, truthfully unable to move, with Benjamin waiting silently beside me.

When the last worshiper had left, Daniel sat on the altar steps with his hands neatly folded in front of him. He watched me, as the acolytes put out the candles. I sat straight and still on the wooden pew, my heart racing mercilessly. Benjamin was peering down at the hymnal in his lap, paging through it thoughtfully. After the acolytes left, Daniel stood and walked slowly down the center aisle to where we sat. He held out a hand to Benjamin.

"I don't think we've met, have we?" he asked warmly.

"No, Father. My name is Benjamin." He looked up at *his father*, unknown to him. I observed all of this as if above somewhere floating, my breathing shallow, my thinking labored. I shouldn't have brought Benjamin. Confronting Daniel hadn't occurred to me when I flew out the door to attend this mass. Observing him from afar was all I meant to do, but something had urged me on, urged me forward to communion, and kept me cemented to the pew as others shuffled out.

"Would you mind, Benjamin, if your mother and I walked over there and spoke in private?" Daniel nodded toward the alcove on one side of the altar area.

"No." Benjamin glanced at me, and then leafed through the hymnal again. I stood on shaky legs and walked down the aisle just in front of Daniel.

When I reached the altar, I hesitated. He touched my upper arm and guided me into the alcove, where I stood between two round pillars in the dimly lit space. My mind was ablaze with questions, twelve years worth. I looked at him, my arms folded defensively in front of me.

"Is this why you never called?"

"Yes."

"Who are you, Daniel? *What* are you?" I felt weak from the emotions welling up inside me, and leaned against a wall in the empty alcove. "An angel? A *demon?*"

"Is that what you think? That I'm a demon?" Slowly he walked over to where I stood.

"No. Of course not. I didn't come here to be unkind." I looked at him closely, his white-blond hair, his chiseled angelic features, still smooth and handsome. "It's just that you . . . overwhelm me with your presence . . . just as you did twelve years ago."

Daniel looked at me intensely with his exceptionally blue eyes. "I do believe in demons, and that there are angels among us . . . such as yourself." He sighed deeply and stared at the pillar beside us. "I'm only a humble priest, Tori. A servant of God . . . a flawed one, I know . . . because you overwhelmed me, too." His expression was vulnerable, pensive. Daniel touched my hair, hesitantly, as if it might break, or maybe he would.

"But there's never been anyone else. You are the only woman I've ever been with."

"Ever?" I couldn't help but look surprised.

"Ever. I have always known I would be a priest. I couldn't let anything get in the way, and so I didn't let anyone be irresistible." He paused, his expression strained. "But you were." Daniel touched my cheek with longing in his brilliant eyes that said perhaps I still was.

How could he have been such a divine lover without *any* experience? Logic told me not to believe him, but my instincts told me otherwise. "So, in a way, I've been *your* demon," I concluded.

Daniel put his hands in the pockets of his robe, purposefully, as if to make himself stop touching me, and glanced at Benjamin, still seated in the sanctuary. I observed our son waiting impatiently on the bench, absentmindedly thumbing through the hymnal.

"Where is his father, Tori?" Daniel's expression turned to one of torment as he looked back at me and studied my face.

"His father chose not to be a part of our lives." I shrugged. My eyes held his with confidence, for surely truer words had never been spoken.

"He looks just like me . . . with that flaxen hair and those intense blue eyes." Panic clouded his beautiful face. "Is he . . . mine?"

"You forget my eyes are also an odd shade of blue, Daniel. Perhaps not the same shade as yours, but not far from it, and I am sure mine were that exact color as a child," I lied. "As for the hair, my brother's was identical to Benjamin's." My gaze upon him did not waver, nor my voice.

"I don't know whether to be relieved or disappointed." He glanced at the boy again. "He is a handsome lad, confident . . . patient. I bet he's quite intelligent and creative, like his mother."

"He is . . . very special," I agreed.

"You recovered quickly from . . . whatever we felt for each other." He didn't look at me.

"It was love, Daniel. At least for me." I paused. "It isn't right to judge others. Isn't that a house motto around here?" I tried not to sound hurt.

Daniel sighed. I thought he looked like a lost child standing there with his hands in his pockets watching his own child, lost to him forever, for all practical purposes.

"You're right, of course. It's wrong of me to judge you. Especially since I . . . I never called, or came by." He leaned against the pillar beside me. "I wanted to," he whispered. "I wanted to so badly. But I couldn't."

"Why didn't you mention you were a priest, Daniel? The whole time on the river you never indicated you were a man of the cloth."

Daniel looked directly into my eyes, where I saw a hint of the remorse present on that last day of our Rogue trip.

"Forgive me, Tori, but I chose anonymity on the rafting excursion because at the time living up to all that was expected of me seemed overwhelming. I needed a short refuge, a retreat, if you will, from the demands placed upon me by the church. And then I met you, causing me to succumb to the pleasures of intimacy. It nearly destroyed what I knew to be my destiny ever since I was a small boy. That's what loving you did to me."

I nodded my head slowly. "Certainly if I had known, if only you had said something . . . then . . ." my words trailed off.

"Then what, Tori?" Daniel ran nervous fingers through his golden hair. "Would we have felt differently? Behaved differently? I'm not so sure. But I've asked myself many times." Daniel stepped closer, close enough to whisper softly in my ear.

"*Do you feel it, Tori?*"

A shiver ran down my spine. "*Yes,*" I responded in a hushed tone. "*But, Daniel,*" I asked, my libido soaring from his breath on my neck, "*if this bond is so strong . . . so special . . . then why did you never call?*"

He had a faraway look in his unusual eyes. "*Because I am what I am.*" He gestured with his hands, encompassing the space surrounding us. "And *this* is what I am, what I *must* be."

Daniel delicately intertwined his fingers with my hair, and I shuddered. Reaching out hesitantly, I ran my hands along his cheekbone. Our lips lingered close together and almost met. The strength of our chemistry clearly reminded me of another time and place, and vaguely, of almost drowning in the rapids. Forcing myself to pull away, I ran from the alcove yelling, "Benjamin!"

He flew off the bench and kept pace just behind me as I sailed through the monstrous oak doors, letting the fractured shades of a setting sun stream into the sanctuary on our way out.

Hours later, long after Benjamin went to bed, I sat at my desk and stared out the window onto the street. I didn't see cars and concrete buildings. I saw fir trees and a pristine flowing river. I saw Daniel's unusual blue eyes filled with slivers of moonlight. I didn't hear horns and sirens. I heard water washing over rocks and through reeds along the shore as we lay beside the Rogue, our flesh precariously entangled.

I glanced down at Benjamin's picture on my desk and reached out with my fingers, tracing the light streak above his head. Then I gasped, startled by my own revelation. I opened the bottom desk drawer and rummaged through pictures kept there. Finally I pulled out a small album of snapshots and paged through it.

There it was, a picture taken by one of the guides our first day on the river. I was standing between Rachel and Miranda. Daniel stood between Robert and Jonathan. I stared at Jonathan for a moment, remembering his attempt at flirting by the fire that first night. If only I'd known what he knew about Daniel. I wondered if they'd stayed in touch, and what Jonathan was doing now. I tried not to consider what he thought of me after Daniel and I reached our fateful moment of no return that summer.

I pulled the picture from the album and held it up to the light. Yes. It was there, the glow above Daniel's head. Barely noticeable, looking like a flaw in the film or a reflection from the sun. I pulled out several more pictures from the Rogue trip with Daniel in them. One was of him alone. I had taken it on the afternoon of the last day. He was leaning against a rock, his golden curls perfectly messy as always, his eyes painfully blue, like a postcard of waters offshore a remote island in the tropics. And there was that soft yellow glow above his head.

Carefully I held the picture beside the one of Benjamin. They were obviously father and son, with the same eyes and hair . . . *and halo.* What could not be seen was how they had the same pure heart, and healing powers. Almost as if they were not entirely of this world. I thought of the sparrow, and of Sarah. Perhaps Benjamin and Daniel were more than just mere mortals with a gift for healing. *Could angels actually exist?*

Even if it were true, I could never prove it any more than I could make Daniel leave the church, or Benjamin give up healing every hurt creature that crossed his path. I shook my head and threw the pictures into the bottom drawer, slamming it shut. I tried to shut my heart and mind as well, to the endless possibilities of what this meant and if the world was ready for such a revelation.

It wasn't, of course. That was the one thing I could be sure of.

Benjamin, the novel, is available at all major booksellers.

acknowledgments

I want to thank my daughters, Sasha and Anna, who have allowed me to invade their private lives with stories formed in the midst of my life touching theirs, and also, for loving me completely despite my many obvious flaws.

I would like to thank my sons, Ryan and Jonathan, who are among my most avid supporters, and are the kind of husband and father every happy story should have. I could not be prouder of the men they have become.

Thank you to my good friend, Dr. Virginia Simpson, for her diligence as my content editor. Ginni is a gifted writer and author of the memoir, *A Space Between*. Because of Ginni and Sasha, each of these stories may shine in their Sunday best!

I would like to give a special thanks and recognition to the graphic designer Ladd Woodland, who designed the front and back cover for Fractured Hearts, and who also happens to be a dear friend.

About the Author

Award winning author Kathryn Mattingly has always had a passion for writing. Her short fiction pieces have received recognition for excellence in Writer's Digest Award Winning Stories, Mind Trips Unlimited, Beacons of Tomorrow and Internationally Yours: Prize Winning Stories. Her work has appeared in Dark Discoveries magazine, Leading Possibilities e-magazine, and The Possibility Place. Kathryn teaches creative writing at a local college. She is inspired by real-life events and places she has lived or traveled. She currently resides in the foothills of Northern California.

Follow Kathryn: penpublishpromote.com

Made in the USA
Middletown, DE
02 December 2023

43997550R00113